Annie's
Mysteries  Unraveled™

Unraveled Tidings

Jan Fields

Annie's®
AnniesFiction.com

Library of Congress-in-Publication Data
Unraveled Tidings / by Jan Fields
p. cm.
I. Title
2015900758

AnniesFiction.com
(800) 282-6643
Annie's Mysteries Unraveled™
Series Creators: Janice Tate and Ken Tate
Series Editors: Shari Lohner, Janice Tate, and Ken Tate
Cover Illustrator: Kelley McMorris

10 11 12 13 14 | Printed in China | 9 8 7 6 5 4 3 2 1

One

Though the calendar showed December was quickly slipping away, the bright sunshine flooding the living room through the front windows certainly didn't feel very Christmassy. Kate Stevens was happy to be able to run to the store without bundling up, but no matter how many holiday displays she passed, it just didn't feel like Christmas. This was her second Christmas in Texas, but this year felt farther from her old home in Maine than ever before. It didn't help that most of her Texas friends were tied up in their own Christmas plans this year. Even her publisher had virtually shut down until after the holidays. After she finished her column for *Hook and Needle Artistry*, she expected to feel happy about having a little free time for the holiday, but now she wished for the distraction of work.

Maybe she'd feel differently once they got the Christmas tree up. Certainly the chill breeze that managed to sneak around the huge pine tree wedged in her front doorway had brought a nip of Texas winter to her front room. And the scent of pine was so strong it nearly made her sneeze.

The tall, tightly wrapped pine tree *should* have fit through the door. At least that was what Peter Matthews kept insisting as he wrestled with the tips of the branches. They seemed insistent upon clinging to the doorframe as if the tree were grabbing for safe purchase with piney fingers. Each inch through the door resulted in a shower of needles, which littered the floor and clung to Peter's flannel shirt.

Kate had dated the handsome police detective off and on since shortly after she'd moved to Texas, a fact that made her feel both happy and terrified in nearly equal measure. It wasn't that Kate couldn't move on from her painful divorce, exactly. Years had passed since then. It was more her fear of making the same mistake twice, no matter how great Peter seemed.

She shook off the dark thoughts as another shower of needles hit the floor. Wrapping her arms around herself to ward off the chill drifting through the door, she asked, "Don't you think that tree is awfully big?"

"It'll be perfect. I looked for the best, fullest tree on the lot," Peter said. Then he grunted as he tugged in another few inches of shedding pine.

"You seem to have found it." As more and more of the tree made it through the door, Kate began to wonder just how much front room she'd have left when the big tree was set up. "Tell me again why *your* mammoth Christmas tree needs to be in my little front room?"

Peter stopped his wrestling for a moment and turned to look at her. "It's *our* tree, and since you don't come over to my place, it needs to be here."

Kate wasn't ready to be alone with Peter in his apartment, which he'd described as a tiny studio, so she decided to deflect attention away from that specific topic. "This sharing of a giant, shedding pine tree is important?" Kate suddenly had an alarming thought. "Is this some Texas courting ritual I don't know about? It doesn't mean we're engaged or anything like that, does it?"

"It definitely does mean something," Peter said. He stopped and stared at her for a moment, his expression serious.

Kate regretted saying anything.

"It means," he continued, deadpanning for effect, "that Christmas is coming."

Kate smiled, relieved.

"And if we were engaged, you'd know it."

Kate felt her face flush. "Fine, then we're back to the tree. Did it have to be so big and ... shed-y?"

He pointed at her. "It's beautiful. Don't be a Scrooge."

Normally Kate adored Christmas. She loved the parties, twinkling lights, and the giddy secrets of gift buying. She even liked the sometimes tacky music and over-the-top Christmas displays in stores. This year wasn't normal. This year she was nearly two thousand miles away from her oldest friends and what little family she had. When Kate had moved to Texas, she'd pictured building new holiday traditions with her college-age daughter, completely forgetting that Vanessa would need to spend at least some holidays with her father and his parents back in Stony Point. Kate thought about the world of Vanessa's grandparents and she understood why her daughter wanted to spend Christmas with them, but that didn't make it hurt less. She had managed to be brave in front of her daughter, but she'd spent nearly an hour crying after Vanessa drove off in her little blue car just one day before.

Peter must have caught the forlorn expression on her face because he dropped the tree and walked over to wrap his arms around her. "I know you miss Vanessa," he said. "But whether or not that ruins this Christmas is up to you. It won't be ideal, but it can still be good."

Kate nodded, her forehead bumping his shoulder. "I know. I'm sorry." She took a deep breath and stepped back. "I'm sure the tree is gorgeous. Let me help you get that monster inside."

"That's my gal."

Between them, they finally managed to haul the tree through the door and carry it to the empty spot in front of the row of windows. Kate always liked to see her Christmas tree sparkling with welcome through the windows. Unfortunately, when they tried to stand the tree up, it quickly became obvious that it was too tall. Kate stuffed down the "I told you so" that tried to bubble up when the top of the tree bent against the ceiling.

"It's not a problem," Peter insisted as they laid the tree carefully back down and began cutting the string that bound the limbs. "I'll just cut some off the base and the lower branches."

Kate eyed the tree dubiously as it seemed to swell with each string cut. "Sure."

As Peter ran out to his truck for the handsaw, Kate headed into the kitchen to make coffee. In an effort to seem less of a Scrooge, she reached to the back of her cupboard and brought out two Christmas mugs.

She'd gotten them years before at the annual Christmas party of the Hook and Needle Club in Stony Point. All of the members had drawn names for gift-giving, and they had the party at the needlework shop where Kate worked. Kate pictured them sitting in the circle of overstuffed chairs where they gathered weekly to work on their projects.

At Christmas these same chairs gave each person the perfect view to watch members unwrap the sometimes wacky surprise gifts. She remembered her friend Alice MacFarlane laughing as Kate opened hers. The two mugs had been nestled in paper shavings, hiding the design on the sides until Kate pulled them out.

The first mug showed Santa wearing the ugliest sweater Kate could imagine; it had caught her by surprise and made her laugh. The second had a certain red-nosed reindeer in an equally ugly outfit, complete with a droopy hat and earflaps. The back of each featured Mrs. Claus, knitting furiously.

"Sorry," Alice had said when the laughter died down. "I

couldn't find any mugs with Mrs. Claus crocheting."

Kate sighed as she set the mugs on the counter and wondered if the Hook and Needle Club members had drawn names this year. She wished she could be there to see what crazy things hid in the packages this time.

Finally, she gave herself a mental shake. *Stop feeling so sorry for yourself!* She stopped to listen to the crashing and muttering from the front room and then stuck her head around the corner. "Coffee break?"

"Coffee!" Peter's tone was horrified. "We're setting up the Christmas tree!"

"And?"

He crossed his arms over his chest and looked at her in amazement. "You drink *coffee* while setting up your tree?"

"Um, the correct answer here seems to be no, so I'm going to go with that. What's the appropriate Christmas tree beverage?"

"Eggnog."

Kate could almost hear the "of course" at the end of his answer. She gave him an apologetic smile. "I don't have any. I could put an egg in your coffee."

He narrowed his eyes. "You're lucky you're so cute. How about hot chocolate?"

"That I have." Kate ducked back into the kitchen and put on a kettle for hot water. She listened to more clunks, rustling, and grumbles from the front room as she watched the pot. She wondered if Vanessa was helping her grandparents pick out a tree right that minute. She pictured her daughter wearing the silly singing Santa hat that she always put on for tree trimming. When they started that tradition, the hat had fallen down over Vanessa's eyes, but the little girl had still insisted on wearing it.

Kate jumped when she felt Peter's arms slip around her. She'd fallen into nostalgia again. "I think that water has boiled enough," he said. "Now come and see the tree."

The floor was littered with the branches Peter had cut, but he'd finally managed to make the tree short enough for the room. The tree was full and beautifully shaped with a top that nearly brushed the ceiling. "It's perfect," Kate said. She pointed at the needles on the floor. "Do you want me to get the vacuum?"

He looked at the mess he'd made as if surprised at the sight. "Right. I'll carry the branches out to the truck." He quickly gathered up an armload of branches and started for the door and then turned toward her. "Do you have ornaments? Wait, I bought some icicles. I'll get them out of the truck." He was out the door before Kate could come up with an answer to his ornament question. She quickly vacuumed up the needles, leaving the vacuum next to the tree to sweep up the needles that were sure to fall as they decorated. Peter darted back in for another load of branches, and Kate walked back to her studio to get the Christmas boxes from the top of the closet.

As always, stepping into her studio gave her a small rush of joy. The dressmaker's form held her Christmas present for Vanessa, a beautiful white denim jacket with crochet sleeves, collar, and trim. Her large worktable held more denim and a wooden bowl piled with skeins of fine blue yarn that Kate planned to use for the sleeveless sweater that would complete the outfit.

At first she'd worried that she'd taken on too big a task to finish by Christmas, but now she had nothing but time since it would be nearly January before Vanessa got back and they exchanged gifts.

When she walked into the living room with her boxes of ornaments, she found Peter carefully hanging strands of silver on the branches. "Don't the icicles go on last?" she asked.

He shook his head. "No. If you wait until last, you're always tired. Then it's too tempting to just fling them on."

"And that would be bad?"

"Catastrophic. You get clumps."

Kate nodded. She picked up a handful of tinsel and flung it at the tree. Some of the strands floated into place nicely, but a fair number hit and clung in a wad.

"Hey!" Peter yelped. Then he looked at her in mock horror. "Don't tell me you're a tree-trimming barbarian."

She grinned in response, snatching up another handful. "I am," she said. "This is the way Vanessa and I always did it." She prepared to toss the second clump, but Peter grabbed her arm, and they wrestled for it.

"As an officer of the law, I insist you lay down the tinsel before you commit a crime against Christmas," he said as she switched hands, trying to get the leverage to fling the tinsel.

She laughed. "I've got tinsel, and I know how to use it."

Eventually, the floor around them was littered with strands of silver that mixed with the scattered needles from the tree. Kate had managed to throw a few more clumps of tinsel at the tree, but far more of it covered the floor, Peter, and her. They were laughing so hard they didn't hear the knock at the door. The door cracked open. "Kate?"

Laughing still, Kate turned toward the door. The second recognition hit her, she whooped and pulled free from Peter to run to the door. "Alice!"

Alice MacFarlane pushed the door open the rest of the way and hugged Kate. They both talked at once, telling one another how great they looked.

"I can't believe this," Kate said. "I was just thinking about you. Why didn't you tell me you were coming?"

"We'd heard you were staying in Texas for Christmas and wanted to surprise you." Alice pulled the scarf from her wavy, dark auburn hair and turned to let Kate see who stood behind her.

Kate smiled at the grizzled man with the warm smile and sparkling gray eyes. "Jim! This *is* a wonderful surprise."

The handsome photographer limped into the house and gave Kate a one-armed hug, gripping the silver head of his cane with the other hand. "We couldn't come to Texas without seeing you. Red wouldn't allow it." Jim pointed at Alice with his thumb.

"Don't let him fool you," Alice said. "He was just as excited about the idea."

Jim reached out and picked a bit of tinsel from Kate's hair. "We seem to have interrupted a Christmas free-for-all."

Alice's gaze swept over Kate's shoulder. "Texas tinsel traditions are certainly interesting. Maybe Jim and I should join in."

Kate felt her face warm as she turned back toward Peter. She noticed the tinsel sparkling from his hair and the shoulders of his flannel shirt. *Oops.* She knew that any explanation she offered would just give Alice and Jim more fuel to tease her with, so she just gestured toward Peter. "Alice, Jim, this is my friend Peter Matthews," she said. "Peter, this is Alice MacFarlane and Jim Parker."

"Peter?" Alice echoed, her eyes lighting up. "The police detective?"

"The very one," Peter said as he offered his hand. As he moved, a piece of tinsel slipped from his sleeve and drifted to the floor. "Kate speaks of both of you often."

"Hopefully not enough to get us arrested," Jim said as he shook Peter's hand.

"You're safe. I'm off duty."

"So, when did you get in?" Kate asked as she swept a hand through her hair and came away with several strands of tinsel. "Are you going to be in Texas long? Are you working on a book?"

Jim laughed. "Now you sound like Alice, with all the questions. Let me see if I can answer them in order: Yesterday afternoon, at least until Christmas, something much better."

"Don't tease," Alice scolded him. Then she turned to Kate. "We're getting married!" This announcement led to another round of hugs and handshakes. Kate admired Alice's ring. Since Alice sold Princessa jewelry, her hands were always full of rings, so Kate had missed the flash of the modest diamond when her friend had first arrived.

"You've come a long way for a wedding," Peter suggested. "Not that Texas isn't romantic and probably a lot warmer than Maine right now, but don't most folks have their weddings where they live?"

Alice's smile slipped away, and she sighed. "Normally, yes, but we have something else we have to do first. When we tried to get our marriage license in Maine, we discovered my marriage to John is apparently not as over as I thought."

Kate looked at her in surprise. "I thought you divorced years ago."

"So did I." Alice shook her head. "That'll teach me not to trust John's choice of lawyers. My lawyer has basically fixed everything now, but I still need John's signature on one document. Jim thought we should come and collect it in person."

"I don't trust the mail or John MacFarlane," Jim said.

"And John's in Texas?" Kate asked.

Alice nodded. "Surprisingly, yes. It took a while to track him down. He moves around a lot and tends to get himself into situations where it's not smart to leave a forwarding address."

"All the better to avoid criminal charges," Jim added. It was clear that Jim Parker was no fan of Alice's ex-husband. Kate wondered if Peter would be like that if he ever met Harry. She shuddered as the image of a meeting between the two men flashed through her mind. It probably wouldn't be pretty.

Alice gave Jim's arm a squeeze. "Thankfully, John promised to sign the paper with no issue. We just have to go over to his apartment later."

"After that, I'm going to marry this woman so fast it'll make her head spin," Jim said. "I'm not risking her coming to her senses."

Alice smiled at him fondly. "Also, with Jim's book schedule, we need to slip in the wedding while we can. Which brings me to my next question. Would you stand up for me at the wedding? With you there, the wedding will still feel like home, even when we're so far away."

"Of course, I'd be delighted," Kate said, grinning. "Though what will everyone in Stony Point think about not getting invited to the wedding?" Kate knew several members of the Hook and Needle Club who were certain to feel a bit slighted.

Alice laughed. "They'll think it's about time I married this old pirate. I'm really hoping for a Christmas Eve wedding."

Kate looked at her friend in shock. "A whole wedding in about a week!"

"Actually, I'm thinking more justice of the peace and a clean shirt than a *whole* wedding," Jim drawled.

"Wow, a clean shirt? You *do* want to go formal," Alice teased. Then her smile slipped away again. "But first, we have to get John to sign the paper."

"You said he already agreed," Kate said, confused by Alice's obvious concern.

"I'm probably worrying over nothing, but it always makes me nervous when John is too obliging. I guess I'm just waiting for the other shoe to drop—the one where he wants money."

"If he wants money, I'll give him money," Jim said seriously. "I'll do whatever it takes to marry you, Alice. And John MacFarlane *will* sign that paper, or I'll kill him and the paper won't matter."

"Whoa," Peter said. "Don't plan any murders in front of me. Remember, I am a homicide detective."

"Oh, don't pay him any mind," Alice said, swatting Jim lightly. "He's just big talk."

"Just talk," Jim said with a fierce smile. "As long as he signs."

Kate felt the strangest chill go up her spine at the expression on Jim's face. She shook her head. *That's just one of those things people say. Right?*

Two

Clearly any reference to John MacFarlane upset Jim, so Kate decided to distract everyone with hot chocolate. Alice followed Kate to the kitchen while Peter picked up tinsel from the floor and chatted with Jim about his work.

"Are you sure having Jim and John in the same room is going to be a good idea?" Kate asked when she and Alice were out of hearing range of the men. "As I remember, John is really good at provoking people."

"We need the paper signed. Jim won't do anything to jeopardize that. I think I can fend off any potential assault charges."

Kate poured hot water into the mugs. "Do you have a special dress for the wedding?"

"Not a traditional gown, but I did buy a lovely jade green silk dress that I haven't had a chance to wear. It's simple, without a lot of fussy details—just long sleeves and a sweetheart neckline."

"That color should be great with your hair."

They carried the mugs out into the living room just as Peter's cellphone rang. He gave Kate an apologetic smile. "Sorry, it's work. I'll need to take this. I promise not to be talked into leaving if at all possible."

"If you need privacy, use my studio."

"Thanks." Peter strode across the room with the phone to his ear.

Kate scooped up the pile of tinsel Peter had left on the coffee table so they would have room for their mugs. "I don't suppose you guys want to help with the tree trimming?"

"I might," Alice said. "It looked like you two were having fun."

"Yeah," Jim said. "You'll have to demonstrate your technique. I'm assuming you test-drive the decorations on each other before putting them on the tree?"

Kate felt her cheeks warm as her friends gave her mischievous grins. Unable to think of anything to say, she stammered for a moment. Alice didn't help at all as she sat and gave Kate an inquisitive look.

It was Peter's return from the studio that saved Kate. "I hate to leave you with the tree undecorated, but duty calls. I need to go." He gave her a quick kiss on the cheek.

"That's all right," Kate said. "I'll probably clean up in here and leave the rest of the decorating until you can help."

Peter brightened at that. "That would be great, if you don't mind."

"I don't mind."

Peter nodded toward Alice and Jim. "It was good to meet you. I hope I'll see you both some more while you're here."

"It seems likely," Jim drawled.

After Peter left, Kate slipped into her favorite crocheting chair and sipped her hot chocolate while Jim and Alice settled on the sofa. "So, when are you guys meeting ... um ...?" Kate wasn't sure she wanted to say John's name again since it tended to work Jim up.

Alice glanced at her watch. "Actually, we should be going if we're going to get there on time, but we'd love it if you'd come to supper with us. We can drive into Fort Worth, get the signature, eat, and have you back home in time for your beauty sleep."

"Are you sure I won't be a third wheel?" Kate asked.

"Definitely not," Jim said. "I've been dragging Alice all over the country with my photo shoots. She's heard all my stories at least three times, though she pretends she hasn't. And she doesn't get nearly enough time with her friends."

"Plus, I wouldn't mind the moral support when we get the paper signed," Alice added. "You can be our calming influence, and we're going to need all of that we can get."

Kate wasn't sure a Zen garden could provide enough calm when Jim and John clashed, but she agreed to go along. Having two good friends show up was an unexpected pleasure. She definitely wasn't ready to see them leave.

When they walked outside, Kate was happy that Alice had the top up on her Mustang convertible for a change. There was a running joke back in Stony Point about Alice stretching top-down season until she risked frostbite. Sage Hills in December wasn't nearly as cold as Stony Point, but Kate knew that the nip in the air could quickly become *really* uncomfortable in an open car.

On the drive to Fort Worth, Alice caught Kate up on things back in Stony Point. Kate was glad to hear all her friends were doing well. She kept up as best she could with phone calls and letters, but still it was nice to talk with someone who knew everybody.

"I got a letter from Annie not long ago," Kate said. "She sounds supremely happy being Mrs. Ian Butler. She said they're putting Ian's house on the market?"

"Yeah, I don't think she was ready to leave all the memories of her grandmother behind by selling *her* house. And Ian seems happy as long as she's happy."

"Smart man," Jim said. Kate smiled. Ian and Jim had clashed more than once over the years, so it was nice to hear him complimenting Ian instead of grumbling about him.

"Well, I'm glad they're doing so well," Kate said.

"They are," Alice agreed. "I missed a lot of the dreamy honeymoon months because of Jim's photo shoots, but I don't think *they* missed *me* much." Then Alice glanced into the rearview mirror with a big grin. "I did have a long, cozy chat with Annie on the phone the other night, and I know the latest scoop on the most important relationship in Stony Point."

"What's that?" Kate asked curiously. She would have thought Annie and Ian were the most important relationship to Alice. After all, she and Annie had been friends since they were kids.

"Boots and Tartan, of course."

Kate burst out laughing. She *had* wondered how Annie's spoiled cat got along with her new housemate. Ian's dog, Tartan, was the most rambunctious schnauzer Kate had ever seen. The combination of Boots and Tartan under one roof must have been explosive. The chubby cat definitely considered herself the queen of the house. "Tell me! Did Boots let the poor dog live?"

"Well, there were some definite dustups," Alice said. "In fact, whenever I'm home, I haul Boots over to my house to give Tartan's poor nose a break from Boots' claws. But I think they've sorted it out now."

"Really?"

Alice laughed. "Of course. Tartan knows Boots is in charge and behaves accordingly."

Jim chuckled at that. "So, he learned the lesson of every smart guy in the world: Life is easier if you let the women have their way."

Alice poked him. "And don't you forget it, buddy."

When they reached the apartment complex on the outskirts of Fort Worth, Jim gave a low whistle. The place was beautiful, with three buildings clustered around a huge pool and gorgeous landscaping everywhere. The apartment buildings themselves were clad in light brick and cream-color clapboard. "I wonder who John robbed this time to get such a nice place," Jim said.

"I don't know," Alice said. "I don't want to know. I just want a signature." She swung her convertible into an empty parking spot and pointed at Jim. "No matter what happens, no fighting."

"I can't promise that, Red," Jim said. He raised his hands as Alice glared. "I promise that I'll behave unless I have no choice."

Alice frowned at Jim for a moment, but she must have decided that she wasn't going to get anything better. "Fine. Choose wisely."

The path up to the building was spotlessly clean. In fact, Kate saw no sign of discarded trash anywhere. A few late-season mums still held white blooms. When they reached the door to John's building, Alice punched in the code to get into the building. The door opened immediately. "One hurdle down."

"You say that like you weren't sure the code would work," Kate said as they walked down the clean, neat hallway.

Alice shrugged. "I have to admit, when we pulled in, I did wonder if John had sent me to the wrong address. But the code he gave me worked. I guess I'm a little paranoid where my ex is concerned."

"Paranoia is smart wherever John MacFarlane is concerned," Jim said. "Paranoia and a big stick."

When they reached the door to John's apartment, Alice gave Jim one more warning look. "Stay calm."

"I'm always calm."

"When you say things like that, it doesn't make me feel comforted. We're not going to get him to sign if you punch him in the face."

"You can't be sure of that."

"Jim Parker!"

Jim just grinned as he reached around her and knocked on the door. They stood and waited, but the door didn't open. Jim knocked again, this time using his cane to rap on the door. The sound rang in the hallway. There was no way that someone inside wouldn't have heard it. Again no answer.

"Great. So much for being too paranoid," Alice said as she stepped up and pounded the door with the side of her fist. "This is just what I expected. He makes an appointment and then stands me up. He probably did it just to make me crazy. It's the story of our whole relationship."

"Maybe he's just running late," Kate suggested hopefully. "Something unexpected could have come up. When did you last talk to him?"

"Yesterday morning," Alice said. "We called from the road just to remind him to be here to sign the paper today."

A voice drifted their way. "If you're looking for my loser neighbor, you won't find him in there. I'm thinking he's dead."

"Dead?" Alice yelped.

"Dead!"

Three

They all looked down the hall toward the outer door. A woman with salt-and-pepper hair and a leathery tan peered at them with a frown. Her arms were full of shopping bags and packages, which she dumped on the floor. Then she patted her pockets, appearing to search for her keys. She glanced toward them again and sighed. "Don't mind me; I'm just indulging in a little wishful thinking."

Jim chuckled as Alice stepped around him and said, "Wishing he was dead? Do you know him that well?"

"Not really, but what I do know, I don't like," the woman said. "It's been real quiet over there since the big row late last night. I figure he's either dead or laying low somewhere. Either one is a plus for me."

"What kind of row last night?" Alice asked.

The woman shrugged as she turned to shove her key into her lock. "Lots of yelling and breaking glass. Woke me from a sound sleep. I was going to call the cops, but then I heard scuffling in the hall, so I looked through my peephole and saw MacFarlane being hustled out by two big men. It looked like the kind of situation where a smart woman doesn't get involved. It was quiet after that, so I went back to bed. I've been out most of the day, so I reckon he could have come back and left again."

"Could you describe the men?" Jim asked.

The woman looked at him blandly. "Big. Scary." She shrugged. "I was looking through my peephole. It doesn't exactly give the best view. And they seemed to be moving MacFarlane along in a hurry."

"Was he bound?" Jim asked. "Were they dragging him? Did they have guns?"

The woman shook her head. "No, he was walking normally, though he didn't seem all that happy. I didn't see any guns. But again, it was a peephole, so I guess there might have been. He didn't look beat up or anything, and he wasn't begging for his life. He looked more annoyed, the way I feel just about every time I deal with that guy." She sighed. "He probably isn't dead, but I don't think he's there either."

Alice groaned. "I should have known something like this would happen. It's like my marriage all over again. Every time I started to think things would look up, John would cheat the wrong person or flirt with the wrong married woman. Then he'd disappear for a while only to turn up eventually, either beat-up or broke."

The woman raised her eyebrows, and her forehead folded into wrinkled pleats. "You were married to that loser? You have my condolences."

Jim huffed, leaning on the wall and crossing his arms over his chest. "So, we wait around Fort Worth until he turns up?"

The woman fiddled with the key ring in her hands, making the keys chime against one another. "Maybe I'll get lucky and he won't come back. I could get a neighbor who doesn't make so much noise and doesn't steal my packages."

"He *stole* from you?" Kate blurted, shocked.

She nodded. "My son signed me up for one of those fruit-of-the-month clubs, only I hardly ever got the fruit. I thought it was a big scam until I found out the packages were being swiped."

"And you know it was him?" Jim asked, nodding toward the apartment door.

"Without a doubt. I caught him red-handed once. He claimed he was just checking to be sure it was delivered to the right door since he was expecting a package too. But I knew he was a lying dog." She snorted and shoved her keys into her pocket. "That's why I hope those goons don't bring him back. Good riddance to bad rubbish."

She turned back to her door and began gathering her packages. "Can I help with that?" Kate asked.

"No thanks, honey. I got them this far; I can get them the rest of the way."

"I have one more question," Jim said, giving her the full wattage of his charming smile. "We really need to get in there. If I were to pick the lock on his apartment, would you call the cops?"

She smiled back. "Go ahead, handsome. Just don't make too much noise while you're in there. And if you see any fancy oranges in the fridge, I'd like to have them back. They probably taste like old shoes, but they were a present from my son, so I'd like to have at least one."

Jim had the lock picked in minutes. Inside, the apartment was starkly modern with clean lines and sharp angles. The color scheme of earth tones with terra-cotta and dark blue accents was virtually the only nod to its Texas location. Overall, the look was pricey but impersonal.

They walked through the open living and dining area. On the floor near the pale sofa, vibrant blue shards from a broken ceramic vase mixed with glass from a picture frame. "Well, we know why she heard breaking glass," Jim said as he poked a shard with the tip of his cane.

Alice pulled her sweater sleeve down over her hand and then picked up the broken picture frame. The photograph in it was of John. He was grinning at the camera and leaning casually against a dove-gray Jaguar, his legs crossed at the ankles. The expression on his face could only be described as a smirk. "Leave it to John to have framed photos of himself as his only decor. Once a narcissist, always a narcissist."

"Everyone likes to look at their best friend," Jim responded wryly. "Especially when it's also your only friend. You ladies poke around out here and see if he left any clue to what kind of trouble he's in. I'll search the bedroom."

"I'll check the bathroom," Kate offered. "You never know what you can learn from a medicine cabinet."

Her first impression of the bathroom was that it was much bigger than the one in her house. Sticky notes covered the edges of the vanity mirror. The notes all had positive affirmations on them, like "You're destined for success" and "Nothing can stand in your way."

Kate opened the medicine cabinet and looked over the contents. She found several disposable razors, a couple spools of dental floss, one bottle of over-the-counter pain medication, and another for allergies. The only prescription medicine was for high blood pressure. "Being an all-around bad guy must be stressful," she muttered.

She glanced toward the toilet. In police shows on television, bad guys often stashed things in the water tank on the back of the toilet. She wrinkled her nose at the thought, but then decided she needed to be thorough. She lifted the heavy ceramic lid and looked inside. She was surprised to find a plastic bag taped to the underside of the lid. Inside, she could see a flash drive for a computer. "Bingo!"

She pocketed the drive, replaced the lid, washed her hands thoroughly, and looked around for anything else. A laundry stain stick was on the counter beside the sink, and a dress shirt hung over a small towel bar. She picked up the shirt. At first she thought she saw blood stains on the collar, but she touched one with her finger and realized it was lipstick.

"Apparently *someone* likes you," she said softly. As she folded the shirt to hang it back on the towel bar, something rustled in the pocket. She pulled out a cocktail napkin. The word "Slammin'" was printed on the napkin, and someone had written a phone number under that in neat block letters.

Kate carried the napkin back into the living room. "I found a lipstick-smeared shirt in the bathroom," she said. "He had this in the pocket. I'm pretty sure Slammin' is a night club." She handed the napkin to Alice.

Alice gave the napkin a glare. "I can't tell you how many napkins with mysterious phone numbers I saw while I was married to that rat. He always had an explanation, and they were always equally unbelievable."

"I also found this." Kate held up the flash drive. "John apparently didn't want anyone to see it since it was inside the tank of the toilet."

Alice wrinkled her nose. "Thanks for searching above and beyond the call." She took the drive and glanced around the large living room and dining room combination. "This is a great find, but I don't see a computer. Maybe Jim will find one in the bedroom."

"Maybe he doesn't have one."

"I'm sure he must. He insisted on keeping up with technology. He said it was the key to success." Alice waved her hand around the apartment. "This is a really nice place. Maybe he finally found the success he wanted so much."

"From what the neighbor said, he also found trouble."

Alice nodded, her face sober. Then she held up a phone. "I found something too."

"He left his cellphone behind?" Kate said. "I guess that proves he left in a hurry with those men."

"I found it under the sofa," Alice said.

"Maybe he dropped it while someone was smashing up his apartment," Kate suggested.

"Maybe," Alice said. "Maybe he dropped it on purpose to keep it out of their hands."

Kate nodded. Everything they found just left them with more questions. "At least we have more phone numbers to check on. We can call around and see if John's with someone he knows."

Alice shook her head. "It's password protected. We won't be calling anyone from this phone unless I can figure out his password."

"Look what I found." They turned to see Jim coming from the bedroom with a file folder in his hand. "It's got photographs. I found it under the mattress on the bed."

Alice wrinkled her nose. "Don't tell me. They're some kind of sordid blackmail photos? Cheating spouses? Drug deals?"

"Nothing like that. Hiding them under the mattress suggests they're important and secret, but I sure can't figure out why anyone would pay blackmail money for them." Jim opened the file to show them the photos of men, trucks, and machinery. The men didn't appear to be aware of the camera and none of them appeared particularly furtive. They looked like perfectly normal photos of some kind of work site; nothing in them looked even slightly suspicious. "Why hide something like this?"

"There must be more to it than it appears," Alice said. "At any rate, we ought to keep them. When John comes back, he might be willing to trade the folder for his signature."

"I don't know," Kate said. "If he's using it to blackmail

someone, do you really want to give it back to him?"

Alice sighed. "I suppose not. We can ask him what it's for and only give it back if it doesn't involve blackmail. Of course, he lies like a cheap rug." She turned back to Jim. "Did you find a computer in there?"

Jim shook his head. "Why?"

"Kate found a flash drive. Why have a flash drive if you don't have a computer?"

"Another interesting question. Maybe his visitors took it when they took him. We'll have to try this in my laptop when we get back to our hotel."

"First, we should probably follow up on Kate's other clue," Alice suggested. Kate showed Jim the napkin.

"Maybe whoever belongs to that number knows where John could be," Alice said. She pulled out her cellphone and punched in the number.

"Hello," Alice said when the call was answered. She immediately switched her phone to speaker mode. "I'm not sure who I'm calling. I found your number on a napkin in John MacFarlane's pocket."

"John MacFarlane?" The shrill female voice on the other end of the call sounded furious. "You can tell him to lose my number!"

"I'll be glad to, if I can find him. Do you have any idea where he might be?" Alice asked.

"Do I sound like his mother?" the woman asked.

"No. But apparently you know him, and I do have a couple of questions. It looks like he could be in trouble. Do you know why?"

"Because he's scum?" the woman said.

"Well, yes, there's that," Alice agreed. "But I was hoping for something more detailed."

"Pond scum?" the woman suggested.

Jim huffed and took the phone from Alice's hand. "Miss? It's important that we find this pond scum. Would you be so kind as to tell us your name?"

"No, I would not. I'll tell you that John MacFarlane is a creep, and that's all I have to say on the subject." At that, she hung up.

"She was helpful," Jim said cheerfully. Then he rubbed his hands together. "All right, did either of you search the kitchen?" They quickly discovered the fridge was mostly empty except for a variety of takeout containers, some fruit in the produce drawer, and half a bottle of red wine. The freezer held a couple of frozen dinners and ice cubes.

"Clearly he doesn't eat in much," Kate said. She reopened the fridge and took an orange out of the fruit drawer. It had probably been a nice piece of fruit, but now it was beginning to shrivel. "Do you think the neighbor wants these back?"

"I wouldn't," Alice answered. "But maybe she'd like them as some kind of proof."

"I'll hang on to one." Kate closed the fridge. The door itself held several magnets advertising local businesses. Scattered among the magnets were more mini pep talks on sticky notes. "Never give up!" "Be a winner!"

Kate tapped one with her finger. "Was he always into stuff like that?"

Alice shook her head. "That's definitely new. He used to say all that positive affirmation stuff was stupid. It's one of the few things John and I agreed on. I think it's important not to talk yourself down, but there is a point where it starts to feel silly."

Jim spoke from the dining room. "It looks like he doesn't think it's stupid anymore." He held up a well-thumbed paperback. "It's on the power of positive affirmations, and it's by someone named Archer Ogilvie." A photo on the back cover showed the author to be a balding man with a wide grin. Jim flipped through the book, shaking his head. "Judging by all the highlighting in this book, your ex thinks this guy is a genius."

He tossed the book back onto the table. "I don't think there's anything else to find here. Looks like we're stuck for now, so we might as well go grab something to eat. We'll just take this folder, the phone, the flash drive, and the napkin Kate found with us."

"Why take the napkin?" Kate asked. "We already called the number. She wasn't exactly helpful."

"She wasn't," Jim agreed. "But someone else at the club might be."

Before they left, Alice pulled a pen and paper from her purse. She began writing a note asking John to call immediately. She looked up at Kate. "My cell coverage has been a little spotty. Can I put your cell number on here too? When he calls, I want someone to get the message."

"That would be fine," Kate said.

Alice stuck the note on the fridge under a magnet advertising a local camera shop. Then they left. "I guess we have to wait for him to get back," Alice said glumly as they closed the door behind them. "That's a little too much déjà vu for me."

"Think of it as active waiting," Jim said. "We have a few clues; maybe we can use them to keep us busy." He winked at her. "After we eat."

"Give me just a second to return this orange." Kate rapped on the neighbor's door. She immediately heard the sound of shuffling feet, and the door soon opened. Kate held out the orange.

The woman took it, turning the fruit over in her hands. "This is one of them, all right. See the mark?" She turned the orange toward Kate to show some of the red printing on the rind. "I don't suppose you found that loser's dead body in there?"

Kate shook her head, and Jim stepped closer. "When you looked out your peephole, you didn't happen to see the men carrying anything, did you? A computer for instance?"

"Maybe." The woman shrugged a single shoulder. "I honestly don't remember. They could have been holding a small computer, like a laptop." The wrinkles in her face deepened as she tried to remember. "I kind of think I remember one of the men holding stuff, but that could be my memory playing tricks just because you asked. I'm sorry."

"No problem," Jim said. "Thanks for looking the other way during our visit."

The woman's face lightened in a smile. "And thank you for the orange. I hope you find the guy. Punch him in the nose for me if you get a chance."

"That I would enjoy," Jim said.

When the woman closed her door, Alice gave Jim a light punch on the arm and then slipped her hand through his arm as they headed out of the building. "Now for food!"

Over nachos, enchiladas, and iced tea in a dimly lit Tex-Mex restaurant, they discussed what their next move should be.

"The photos and flash drive are the most interesting things we found," Jim said. "But these photos sure don't offer many clues." He flipped through the pictures again and shook his head. "You can't even see the whole logo on the truck doors. One of these trucks has a mismatched mud flap, but that wouldn't help much unless we knew where to look for the truck."

"It would stand out though," Kate said, leaning over to take a closer look, "since the mismatched flap is purple."

"I guess that's something." Jim sighed.

Alice nodded as she scooped up fresh salsa with a chip. "Of course, the men in the pictures could be minor celebrities in Fort Worth. We have no way to know." She turned to Kate. "Do any of them look familiar? Maybe from the news?"

Kate looked through the photos again and shook her head. "I could show them to my neighbor," she suggested tentatively. "She does event planning for the Hamilton Arms Hotel in Fort Worth. It's upscale and hosts a lot of business functions. If any of the men are well-known locally, Vivi would probably recognize them." Vivi Lawrence was Kate's closest friend in Texas, and she had made it plain in the past that she loved the idea of being involved in the adventures that kept coming Kate's way. Kate felt a smile tug at the corners of her mouth as she thought about her energetic friend. She knew Alice and Vivi would hit it off right away; they were much alike.

"That's a good idea," Jim agreed. "Though we may want to hold off a little. We didn't exactly obtain the photos legally, so the fewer people who know about them, the better." Then he turned to Alice. "Though it might not be breaking and entering since technically you are the man's wife."

Alice looked aghast. "I wish you wouldn't say things like that. I'm trying to eat."

"So, back to keeping the whole breaking and entering secret." He pointed at Kate with the edge of a photo. "That includes not telling your cop boyfriend."

Kate frowned. "Peter's not exactly my boyfriend. We're just friends."

"Oh no," Alice said with a chuckle. "It's the Annie Dawson

effect all over again. She and Ian Butler were 'just friends' right up until the wedding."

Kate shook her head. "This is not the same."

"Of course not," Alice teased. "I saw how Peter looked at you, Kate. He's not *just friends* with you. At least Ian was subtle. Peter gives you calf eyes every time he looks at you."

"I have to agree with Red," Jim said as he reached out to cover Alice's hand with his own. "As a guy who's been smitten with a gorgeous Stony Point woman for years, I know the signs. Your detective is definitely smitten."

Kate felt her cheeks warm in a blush. "I guess we're not *just* friends, but we're not exactly more either." She sighed. "It's complicated." She took a sip of her tea and winced at how sweet it was. She'd discovered that some restaurants took the "sweet" part of the description more seriously than the "tea" part.

"Love is *always* complicated," Jim said.

Kate held up her hands. "Whoa. Neither one of us is ready for the 'l' word."

Jim laughed. "What is it with Stony Point women? A guy's got to sneak up on you, or you run like rabbits."

Alice gave him a playful punch. "I'm no rabbit, buster."

"But you have to admit, you gave me a run for my money. Why else would I be in Fort Worth? I have to marry you quick before you slap me with a 'just friends' label."

Alice gave him a mock scowl. "You keep talking like that and you'll be lucky to stay friends."

Jim took her hand and kissed the back of it. "Whatever you say." Then he turned to Kate with a smile. "But seriously, mum's the word to Peter about the particulars of our search for the scumbag."

Kate nodded, glad the conversation was turning away from

her love life. She'd be happy to keep the whole apartment experience secret. Breaking and entering with old friends wasn't likely to be high on Peter's approved behavior list.

Alice reached over and plucked the napkin they'd retrieved from the apartment out of Jim's pocket. "I say we go here after supper. If John was a regular, we may find someone who knows him well enough to know what kind of trouble he might be in."

Jim raised an eyebrow. "It sounds like a dance club. You sure you're not just looking for a chance to go dancing? You know I'm not exactly Fred Astaire anymore." He patted his pant leg as he spoke. Years before, when Jim was a war correspondent, he'd lost his legs when a bomb brought a building down around him.

Alice grinned back at him. "I don't think you were *ever* Fred Astaire. I see you more as the Gene Kelly type—less debonair, more bandit."

"I'll take that. Just don't expect me to trip the light fantastic," Jim said as he pulled out his smartphone and looked up the club named on the napkin. It wasn't very far away, so after they finished supper, they headed over.

As they drove through the downtown streets, Kate admired the Christmas lights strung everywhere. Each tree they passed twinkled against the night sky. Buildings were draped with lighted garlands. Yet despite the clear signs of Christmas around them, the weather still felt more like autumn to Kate.

The big converted warehouse that held Slammin' showed no sign of recognizing the holiday at all. No garland draped the building, and the only lights outside were neon. When they walked through the doors, Kate saw the bouncer glance at them with an amused smile. She could see why. Their conservative clothing stood out starkly among the skin-baring fashions on the people around them.

The club contained just about everything Kate didn't like in one building. It was dark except for disconcerting flashes of light. It was loud. And it was crowded.

She stuck close to Alice and Jim as they moved through the crowd. The sea of people hopped and gyrated as they bellowed conversation at one another. The air smelled so strongly of heavy perfume and close human contact that Kate could barely breathe.

Kate resisted the urge to cling to the back of Alice's jacket, not wanting her friend to know how panicky the crowd made her feel. Moments later, she wished she *had* held onto Alice when a surge of people slipped between her and her friends. Kate was pushed along by the crowd like a clump of seaweed in the ocean surf. She pressed against the tide of the crowd, but she couldn't find her friends.

Kate stretched, standing on her toes and looking around anxiously. She could not imagine a place where she was more out of her element. And now she was lost to boot.

Again and again strangers bumped into her, making her stumble. She had a sudden mental picture of herself falling to the floor to be trampled, unnoticed. Panic made her feel as if the crowd weren't leaving her enough room to breathe. She just wanted out, but where was the door? All she saw were bodies and more bodies.

She stood precariously on her toes again and caught an especially hard elbow to the back at the same moment someone slammed into her sideways. She lost her footing. She was going down as the crowd surged around her.

Four

Before she could hit the floor, a hand wrapped around her upper arm and jerked her hard to her feet. A young man with a face full of metal piercings leaned close to her ear. "Watch out, man!" Then he let go of her arm, and the crowd washed between them. *Did he really think I was a man?* She glanced down at her crochet sweater and decided the young man must have lost his mind.

The music boomed so loudly that Kate could feel the bass thumping in her chest. She could barely see three feet around her with the flashing lights and crowds of constantly moving strangers. She tried to slip through an opening between two people, but someone ran into her from behind, causing her to stumble forward again. She tripped over her own feet and landed in the arms of a very amused man in a dark suit. "Hello," he said, leaning close to her ear so she could hear.

Kate backpedaled, hoping to put some space between herself and the stranger, but someone else bumped into her. The stranger put a steadying hand on her arm. "Let me get you out of this crowd," he said, again leaning so close that she felt the tickle of his breath against her skin as he spoke in her ear. She nodded since she didn't have much choice; she certainly wasn't going to find Jim and Alice again on her own.

The stranger put an arm around her and moved fluidly through the crowd. Though he wasn't tall or particularly physically imposing, the dancers parted quickly for him as they had *not* done for Kate. In the flashes of light, she saw the man was blond with closely cropped hair. He was older than much of the crowd, probably over forty. Though he wasn't bulky, Kate could feel the hard muscle of his arm through his suit. This was *not* a man she felt comfortable with, and she wasn't going to let him lead her very far.

Because the crowd responded to him by moving out of his way, they were able to reach an open space quickly. Kate assumed the man would let her go then, but he led her up a small set of stairs to a table that sat alone on a platform above the crush of the crowd. "You are above the fray here," he said. He didn't shout, but his voice was big and deep and cut through the bedlam around them. His words were slightly accented, though Kate couldn't have said what country colored them. "Now you can breathe."

Kate's face felt like she might spontaneously combust, and she knew she must have been blushing. She hoped the stranger didn't think her falling on him had been some kind of invitation. She smile nervously. "Thank you. I need to find my friends." But the music and the crowd noise drowned out her words.

"What?" The man leaned toward her so she could speak into his ear, and she repeated her comment. He nodded and spoke again, this time leaning toward her. "You should be able to see them from here. And they can see you. Would you care to sit?"

She didn't care to sit, but standing on the platform felt awkward, so she nodded. He held a chair out for her and then took the chair beside her. "So, tell me," he said in her ear again, "what brings you to this club? You do not seem happy here. I think you are not really fond of clubbing."

"I'm looking for someone."

He gestured to take in the whole crowd. "Almost everyone is."

Kate tipped her head toward him and spoke loudly. "No, I'm looking for someone specific—John MacFarlane. Do you know him?"

The stranger froze, and his intense stillness felt somehow menacing to Kate as he watched her with icy blue eyes. Then the moment passed, and he visibly relaxed before shrugging. "I am afraid I don't."

Kate smiled slightly. "You're better off. I don't know him all that well, but he's not very nice."

"And you are a very nice lady. This I can tell. Why would you look for a man who is not?"

"My friends and I need him to sign a paper."

"An important paper?"

"It's important to my friend."

The stranger nodded. "Then I hope you find him." He waved his hand around the crowd. "He may be here somewhere. Who knows? You would be looking for a needle in a very large stack." He smiled slightly. "The holidays make lonely people want to connect. If this man you are looking for is lonely, perhaps he is here in the crowd. But how would you find him?"

Kate looked over the crowd. People seemed constantly on the move, giving the impression of a single sea of humanity. If she truly focused, she could make out individuals, but it was difficult. The poor lighting and the movement made each person blend into the next. She wondered if Jim and Alice were having better luck.

She glanced at the man beside her. His eyes swept over the crowd. His suit was neat and perfectly tailored. Her eyes drifted to his hands. His fingers were long, and he sported a flawless manicure. He didn't look like a man given to hard work, but still she felt as if she were sitting next to some kind of predator. *He clearly recognizes John's name. So why lie about it? Could he be involved with John's disappearance?*

The stranger seemed uninterested in more conversation. His gaze didn't stray from the shifting crowd until a server in a short skirt and skintight tank top scurried up to the table. The stranger ordered a drink. He looked at Kate, one eyebrow raised in question. She shook her head, and the stranger waved the server away.

Kate folded her hands together. She wondered if she should brave the crowd again. A surge of relief that made her feel weak swept over her when a familiar gravelly voice shouted her name. She turned sharply in the direction of the voice. Alice and Jim stood at the bottom of the flight of stairs. A big man in a tight black T-shirt blocked their way, his gaze turned up toward the man beside Kate.

"Those are my friends," Kate said as she stood.

"And you are Kate," the stranger said, smiling. "I heard the man shout for you. You look like a Kate."

"I hope that's good," Kate said.

"It is lovely." The stranger signaled to the bouncer, and Alice hurried up the stairs. Kate practically flung herself at Alice, who hugged her.

"Sorry," Kate said.

"We thought we'd lost you," Jim said when he reached the platform. "Alice has been scolding me ever since."

"Would you all like to join me for a drink?" the stranger asked them. He held out his hand to Jim. "I am Serge Vasin."

Jim glanced at Kate's face and then shook Vasin's hand, offering his usual easy smile. "No, but thank you for the offer. We appreciate you rescuing our friend. After dragging her here, we felt bad about losing her."

"I could see she does not like the crowd. You should take her home."

"Good idea," Jim said agreeably.

Vasin turned to Kate with a smile. "Like a flower blooming in the snow, you have brightened my barren night. I am glad to have met you, Miss Kate ...?"

Kate felt the blush burn her cheeks again. "Stevens. It was nice to meet you too, Mr. Vasin." She thanked him again for the rescue as she edged toward the steps. The sooner she was out of the club, the happier she'd be.

At the bottom of the stairs, Alice linked arms with Kate. "No losing you this time."

The bouncer had gone up the stairs as they came down. Now he hurried after them and bellowed, "The boss said to help you get to the door. It's a wild crowd tonight."

Jim nodded toward the platform. "Your boss is an interesting man."

The bouncer barked out a laugh from so deep in his chest that it reminded Kate of a sea lion. "You could say that. Let me get you folks out of here."

Earlier, Vasin had moved through the crowd with Kate as if by magic, the sea of people parting respectfully in front of him. Following the bouncer was more like trailing behind an icebreaker. He simply plowed people out of his way, and they darted through the space behind him before the crowd could close in again.

Once they were outside, the bouncer quickly wished them a good night.

Kate spoke before he could rush away. "Is it always like that in there?"

The bouncer smiled down at her. "Usually a Tuesday night isn't so crazy, but people have more free time when the holiday is here." He shrugged. "And everyone is probably lonelier too. Holidays can be hard."

Kate had to agree with that. She thanked the man as he turned to go back into the club.

"Well," Alice said, "*that* was an experience you don't get in Stony Point."

Kate shuddered. "It's one I could do without in the future. Experiences like that remind me why I'm happy with my quiet life. I'm definitely not a city girl. I'm sorry I messed everything up though. I hope you didn't spend the whole time looking for me."

"We asked questions while we looked for you, but we didn't learn anything," Alice said glumly. "You can't really have much of a conversation in a place like that. Jim gave out a few business cards to the waitstaff, but that's about all. The most we can hope for is that someone will call us back."

"I asked Serge Vasin about John," Kate said. "He reacted to the name, but then he pretended he didn't know him. I didn't want to push. Honestly, he scared me a little."

Jim nodded. "I don't think you're the only one who is afraid of Vasin. I wonder if he's the reason no one would admit to knowing John. I asked some of the cocktail waitresses. They all said they didn't know him, but some of them definitely reacted as if they did. They seemed scared, and I couldn't get anything out of anyone. It was too loud to do much talking."

"The famous Jim Parker charm only works on women if they can hear him," Alice added.

"I think I'm a little too old to charm most of the waitstaff in there."

"Your charm knows no age limit," Alice assured him as she linked her arm in his.

"Thanks for your vote of confidence, though I'm fairly sure I'm old enough to be the father of most of them." He herded them toward the club's parking lot. "Let's hope someone's memory comes back later."

As they drove back to Sage Hills, Kate could tell Alice and Jim were making a concerted effort to keep conversation light. She felt a little silly about her panic inside the club. "I hope you're going to include me in any investigating you do tomorrow," Kate said as they began winding through the streets of Sage Hills.

Alice glance at Kate in the rearview mirror. "Really? I thought you'd probably had enough. The club was a little intense."

"It was pretty far out of my comfort zone," Kate admitted. "But I'm fine. I wasn't even lost all that long. Really, I want to help. Unless you're just going to wait until John calls you."

"I don't know that we can assume John will call us. If he's run into trouble here, he may bolt from Texas entirely as soon as he can. That's his MO, as your handsome detective would say."

Jim reached over to squeeze Alice's free hand. "We'll find him before he can do that. Once we get back to the hotel, we'll see if there are any clues on that flash drive."

"We're almost at my house. Why don't you come in?" Kate said. "We can use my laptop. I have to admit, I'm curious to see what's on the drive."

"Are you sure?" Alice asked. "It's getting late, and as I remember, you're not really a night person."

Kate yawned and clamped a quick hand over it. "Ignore that. I do want to see. Please come in."

They stayed long enough to discover the flash drive was password protected, just like the phone. "I'll take it to the hotel," Alice said, "and see if I can brainstorm some passwords John might have used."

"Like 'loser'?" Jim asked.

Alice laughed. "Accurate but unlikely. Do you want us to swing by in the morning when we've come up with our next move? We don't want to crash any plans you and Peter might have."

"I think he's working," Kate said tentatively. "But if he calls, I'll let you know. I assume we'll be finishing the tree decoration eventually."

"You don't sound very happy about that," Jim observed, his thick gray eyebrows drawn together in concern.

"I am fighting the urge to feel sorry for myself," Kate admitted. "Vanessa is in Stony Point with Harry and his folks. I miss her. All my usual Christmas activities revolve around being a mom. Plus, some of the friends I've made here through my crocheting are out of town as well." She gave a small laugh. "Even my favorite yarn shop hired new help so the owner could go out of town with her husband *and* my agent! I guess I feel a little abandoned."

Alice gave her a quick hug. "Then we'll just have to keep you busy. It'll be like old times with a mystery to solve."

Kate managed a smile. "That should help."

As soon as her friends left, Kate tidied up the living room and let the stress of the evening melt away so she could get to sleep. She smiled as she piled handfuls of tinsel into a box to wait until Peter wanted to come over for more tree trimming. Then she checked on the water level in the tree stand. The poor Christmas tree looked sadly bare in the dim light of the front room with only glints coming from the wads of tinsel Kate had flung at it earlier. When Kate took a deep breath, the pine scent brought a wave of nostalgia and homesickness that made her tear up.

The phone rang, and Kate jumped with surprise. She glanced at the clock and saw it was after midnight. Who would call her so late at night? Her mother used to say that "nothing good" made folks call after midnight. Kate had always found that to be true. As she walked to the table where she'd left her purse, she whispered a prayer of safety for Vanessa.

She pulled the phone out of her bag but didn't recognize the caller's number. "Hello?"

A cool, whispery voice spoke one line before the caller hung up: "Curiosity killed the cat. Stay safe, little kitty."

Five

Kate stared at the phone in her hand, puzzling over the vaguely threatening call. Had they upset someone already? And if so, why call her instead of Alice or Jim? After all, Jim was the one handing out his business cards. Then she remembered Serge Vasin asking for her name, and a shiver ran through her. *Could he possibly have gotten my number? How would he?* As she rubbed her chilled skin, she wondered if the club owner had more resources than she'd expected.

"It might not have been the scary man," she told herself softly. The caller had whispered so softly that Kate couldn't even be sure whether it was a man or a woman. "It might have been a prank." Still, the thought of Vasin's coldly appraising eyes chased away any remnants of drowsiness.

Kate sighed. No point in going to bed anytime soon. Instead, she headed for her studio and Vanessa's Christmas present. If she was going to be scared half to death, she might as well do something useful at the same time.

It was nearly two in the morning before Kate finally relaxed enough to head to bed. She had all the sewing done on the matching denim skirt for Vanessa's Christmas gift and had begun the sweater that would complete the set. She gave in when she couldn't keep track of her counting as she worked.

Though she expected to oversleep after staying up so late, Kate woke with the sun on Wednesday morning. As she fixed her morning coffee, she decided to do a little investigating of her own. She retrieved her laptop from her studio and settled down in the kitchen with her coffee.

A search for the name "Serge Vasin" returned mostly puff pieces about the man's philanthropic ventures. She found photos of him in formal dress at a variety of fundraisers. As she looked over the photos, she had to admit that Vasin was a handsome man. She also noticed he often was pictured with extremely beautiful women.

From what Kate could tell as she clicked link after link, Vasin was vitally concerned about hunger in America, obscure diseases, the art scene in Fort Worth, the opera, and the preservation of the Texas blind salamander. *He certainly stays busy.*

As she read a caption under a photo that showed a gorgeous actress hanging adoringly on his arm, she heard a knock at her front door. Actually, it was more of a muffled thump. Kate trotted to the door, eager to share what she'd learned with Jim and Alice.

She opened the door to find Vivi juggling a large box of doughnuts and a plump bag from Once Upon a Yarn, the needlework shop that was Kate's home away from home. Vivi smiled brightly. "I'm sorry to come over so early. I really need your help with the sweater for my mom. With Paige out of town until after Christmas, I didn't know where else to turn." Paige Bryant was the owner of Once Upon a Yarn and a good friend. Vivi held up the box of doughnuts. "Do you have time to help? I've come with a bribe."

"I'm always happy to help," Kate said as she swung open the door. "You didn't need to bring a bribe."

"Shh," Vivi said. "I'm using this as an excuse to eat doughnuts. Though I really do need your help. I've crocheted myself into a mess on the sleeves."

Kate took the box. "Let me put these in the kitchen. We'll fix the sweater, then nosh on doughnuts as our reward."

Vivi followed Kate into the kitchen and glanced at the laptop where the photo of Vasin and the actress remained. "Oh, do you like Jenny Murray? I thought she was fantastic in her latest movie."

"Actually, I was looking at the page to learn more about him."

"Serge Vasin?" Vivi turned round eyes on Kate. "Why would you want to know more about a mobster?"

It was Kate's turn to look surprised. "He's a mobster? All the things I found on the Internet make him sound like a saint."

Vivi shrugged. "The mob thing is just a rumor, though I believe it. He's a scary-looking guy. So intense. I've never been to that club of his, but I have friends from work who've gone once or twice. I have to admit, I was tempted to join them. I love to dance, but that place sounds like it might be a little too wild for me."

"It's very crowded," Kate agreed. "I'm surprised it isn't a violation of some fire code. I could barely breathe in there."

Vivi's eyes widened even more. "*You* were at Slammin'?"

Kate explained about Alice's search for her ex and how it took them to the dance club. At the end, Vivi continued to look at her in total amazement. "I can't believe I know someone who has actually talked to Serge Vasin. What's he like?"

"Very polite," Kate admitted. "And a little scary."

"Really? What did he say?"

"It wasn't anything he said. He was actually very nice to me. I was about to have some kind of panic attack in that crowd. There's just something about him that feels dangerous. Also, after I got home, I got a scary phone call." She described the spooky voice on the phone and the warning it gave her.

"That's kind of vague," Vivi said. "Did it sound like Vasin?"

"Not really. The caller was whispering. I couldn't tell if it was a man or a woman."

"You know, the call might not have anything to do with Vasin or your friend's ex. Maybe some kids are playing pranks. I get those kind of calls sometimes during the holidays. Kids are out of school and staying up late. It could be teenagers at a sleepover or something like that."

"Maybe," Kate said. She would have liked to think the call was just bored teenagers picking numbers at random.

"Do you think your friend's ex might be involved with Vasin?" Vivi asked.

"We don't know, but someone hustled John out of his apartment. The neighbor saw that. And Vasin definitely reacted to John's name when I brought it up. I'm sure I didn't imagine that."

Vivi shook her head. "It sounds like he could be involved with some very bad people. I hope he's all right."

They walked back out to the front room and settled down on the floral love seat to work on Vivi's sweater. Kate quickly found the spot where Vivi had gone astray. "I'm going to have to unravel some of this," she said.

Vivi covered her eyes. "I can't watch. Go ahead though. I want to get this right."

As Kate pulled out the stitches, she admired the unusual yarn. It was pale gray with flecks of other colors woven into the strands. "I haven't seen this yarn at the shop. I need to go in and drool over Paige's yarn selection, but it never seems to be as much fun when she's not there." Kate loved Once Upon a Yarn; the shop carried so many beautiful things that Kate never walked out without fresh inspiration. It reminded her of A Stitch in Time, the yarn shop that had been her home away from home in Maine.

"Paige was unpacking a yarn shipment when I visited last weekend, and I bought all of this color that she had. Mom gets cold on her morning walks, and I thought she'd like a nice cozy sweater. And with all the flecks of color, she could wear it with anything." Vivi sighed and took her hands away from her eyes. "But I may have been a little optimistic."

"Not at all," Kate said. "You just made one mistake, really. I think you can handle the project." For the next few minutes, Kate went over the crochet pattern with Vivi.

"Thanks, I think I got it," Vivi said finally as she took the sweater back and began working. "So, what are you working on for Christmas? I know it has to be something amazing."

"I'm making an outfit for Vanessa, but I have to admit that my heart's not in it as much as usual. I miss her so much. I'm glad I moved here so I can be close while she's in college, but I guess I didn't think it through. I don't like having her so far away during the holidays—especially Christmas."

"Sounds tough," Vivi said.

"And this business of trying to track down Alice's ex brings up a lot of old emotions from my years with Harry. We had some good times when we were married, but so much of it was messed up by his drinking and fits of rage. Now, with Vanessa going to spend Christmas with him ... well, it feels like he's still messing up my life."

"Except that leaving is what children *do* when they grow up," Vivi said. "Who knows where she'll go in the future? She'll get a job. Maybe she'll get married and start a family of her own. Maybe even one a long way from where you live."

"Thanks, pal, that made me feel much better."

"Sorry, I just meant that it's not really fair to blame Harry for that."

Kate nodded. "I know. I just didn't expect Vanessa's growing up to be so soon."

"No matter when it happened, it would be too soon,"

Vivi said. "Now, let's talk about something more fun. How are things with Peter?"

Kate laughed. "Peter's in holiday mode. He wants to build traditions with me, but that really seems like a big step forward. I'm barely handling the idea of stepping back into the dating minefield, much less anything more serious."

"I thought you were over your ex," Vivi said as she worked the crochet hook carefully through a short row. "Aren't you ready to move on?"

"I *have* moved on. I've moved on to making a life that's just mine. I care about Peter, and he's made his feelings very plain. But when Jim—Alice's fiancé—called him my boyfriend, I felt this emotional resistance."

Vivi wrinkled her nose. "I can't totally blame you for that. I hate the term 'boyfriend' for grown-up dating anyway. We need a whole new term, like 'hug buddies' or 'snuggle pies.'"

"'*Snuggle pies*'?" Kate giggled. "I can just see the look on Peter's face if I called him my 'snuggle pie.'"

Vivi joined in the laughter. "Well, if you try it out, snap a photo. I want to see." She glanced down at her wrist and yelped. "Oh no, where has the time gone? I didn't even eat a doughnut, and I have to run. Holiday time at the hotel is nonstop. It seems like all the really big companies want us to do their holiday parties, so I have a zillion details to nail down today. I love to be busy, but this is nearly enough to make my head spin. I'm working like crazy so I can clear my plate enough to spend Christmas with Mom."

"Do you want to take the doughnuts with you to eat in the car?" Kate asked.

"Maybe just one," Vivi said as she followed Kate into the kitchen. "Actually, two," she said as she reached into the box.

They both startled as Kate's phone rang. Vivi finger-waved

and let herself out while Kate went after the phone. She saw that the call was coming from her ex's phone. Certain it must be Vanessa, she answered with a cheery, "Hi, sweetie."

"Well, hello, love."

The deep voice on the phone was definitely not Vanessa, and Kate's smile slipped away. "Oh, Harry. Sorry, I thought Vanessa was calling."

"She left early to go shopping with my mother," Harry said. "I wanted to call and thank you for letting her come up to spend Christmas with us. I know it couldn't have been easy for you."

Kate sighed. "Harry, it wasn't my decision. Vanessa isn't a child. She's in college. She can drive. She decides where she'll spend her time, and she picked Stony Point."

Harry chuckled. "Don't pretend you couldn't have changed her mind if you'd tried. I was always a little jealous of how close you two are."

Kate swallowed the urge to suggest it was his own fault that he didn't have a closer relationship with his daughter. He was always caught up in his work or his drinking—not to mention his love of control. But those were all arguments they'd had many times, and Kate didn't want to start a fresh fight over stale subjects. "Vanessa loves you."

"I know. She's a great kid. You did a terrific job raising her."

Kate's eyes narrowed. She wondered what was bringing on all the compliments. "Are you drinking?"

"What? No! I don't have to be drinking to recognize my own shortcomings." He was silent for a moment. "Look, I didn't call to fight."

"Why *did* you call?"

"Like I said, to thank you for letting Vanessa come visit."

Kate didn't bother to argue again. "You're welcome."

"So …" Harry paused again. "I hear you're seeing someone special."

And now we get to the real point. "I'm not going to discuss
my personal life with you any more than I expect you to
discuss yours with me."

"No, no, of course not. I just … he's a lucky guy."

Kate groaned. *Why does talking with Harry always have
to be so complicated?* "Thanks. Anything else?"

"Now I've ticked you off. I didn't mean to do that."

"I'm not angry. I appreciate your call, but I have to get
going. I have some things to do. Have a good time with
Vanessa and send her my love."

"Right. I will. Merry Christmas, Kate."

"You too, Harry."

When she got off the phone, Kate settled back in front
of her computer with a fresh cup of coffee and a doughnut,
ready to do something productive and shake off the weirdness
of Harry's call. She continued to search for articles related to
Vasin or the club. Another doughnut later, she still hadn't
found anything that hinted at a connection between the
club and organized crime.

She finally stood and carried her cup to the sink. She
was licking cinnamon sugar from her fingers when she heard
another knock at the door. This time it *was* Alice and Jim.

Alice grinned at her sheepishly. "We overslept. I can never
figure out hotel alarm clocks. Then *someone* just had to have
the free breakfast. Lots of it." Jim just gave her a lopsided grin
in response to her remark. "On the upside, we have a lead."

"Great! I have some interesting information too," Kate
said as she led the way back to the kitchen.

Jim spotted the doughnut box and headed straight for it.
Alice moaned. "You cannot possibly be hungry."

"Doughnuts aren't about hungry." He sank his teeth into a doughnut and flecks of cinnamon sugar mixed into the gray of his beard. Alice brushed at them as they looked at Kate's computer and listened to what she'd learned about Vasin.

"So we know Vasin is big into charity functions," Kate said, "and he is rumored to be connected to organized crime."

"It's possible that our lead and your lead are related," Jim said. "We got a phone call this morning from one of the young ladies who took my card last night at the club. She said she had some things to tell me about John but wouldn't say them over the phone."

"You up for it?" Alice asked. "We're meeting her at her apartment. She said any time before noon would work.

"Absolutely," Kate said. "This is a fantastic distraction." For a moment, she wondered if she should tell Alice and Jim about her own phone call. The more she thought about it, the less likely it seemed that the vague warning was real. The whole curious-cat remark sounded more and more like a prank. *It would be silly to take the prank seriously. Right?*

Six

Kate's musings about the strange phone call must have taken a bit too long because she saw Alice look at her sympathetically, misinterpreting the look on her face and the long pause. "Still bummed about Vanessa?"

"I'll get over it," Kate said. For an instant, she thought about telling Alice about her weird call from Harry; at least it wasn't particularly ominous. But then she decided that doing so would only encourage her friend to tease her about Peter. Her feelings for Peter were too confusing to stand up to much teasing, so she just smiled. "I should be back to normal right around the first of January, when Vanessa gets back."

Jim's face turned serious. "Just don't skip the Christmas you *could* have just because you can't have the Christmas you want."

Alice looped an arm through his and leaned against him. "Don't lecture."

Jim held up both hands. "No lecture here. I just know how it feels to kick yourself later when you let something good get away."

"Like all the good things about being alone for Christmas?" Kate asked, wincing slightly at her own mildly whiny tone.

"Like *not* being alone for Christmas. You've got your detective friend, who is clearly smitten with you. And you have Alice and *me*." He puffed out his chest. "I can't believe anyone would overlook the joy of having us around."

Kate smiled. "It *is* pretty amazing to have you here."

"Darn straight," Jim said.

Kate laughed at his expression. "You're right. I'm being a whiner. I'm turning over a new leaf right now." She mimed flipping something over. "How could I possibly be mopey with you and Alice around? I'm ready to dive into our search for a Christmas wedding."

"That's the spirit!" Alice said.

Then Kate remembered something. "Oh, the flash drive! Did you get a chance to plug it into your laptop and try out passwords?"

"Yeah," Jim said grimly. "We couldn't figure out the password."

"You weren't much help," Alice said, giving him a severe look.

He shrugged and then dropped his voice to a conspiratorial tone as he told Kate, "Red took over before I even finished trying all the synonyms for 'deadbeat.' I thought I was on a roll."

"Don't encourage him," Alice warned her.

Jim's mischievous grin slid away. "Unless we can figure out the password, we're stuck."

"And the phone?"

"Same problem," Alice said. "You'd think it would be easy, but I've tried the name of John's first dog, his favorite food, his birthday, his middle name, his mother's name, his father's name, even the names of his favorite bands from the '70s. Nothing."

"We even tried all the synonyms for money," Jim said, "since that's the guy's first love. Actually, second love. He's his own first love."

"You might figure it out yet," Kate said.

"I haven't given up," Alice replied, "but sometimes an idea comes to you while you're doing something totally different. So let's go do something totally different and talk to the woman who called Jim."

"Sounds like a plan," Jim said. "I'll bring the doughnuts."

When they reached the Fort Worth apartment complex, they found it was considerably less upscale than John's. The tiny pool was surrounded by cracked cement and faded lounge chairs. The three buildings that made up the complex all had their backs to the pool, giving each apartment a view of the slightly milky water.

They knocked on the door, and a tall, athletic-looking blonde, who appeared to be in her late twenties, opened it. Her hair was tousled, with dry, frizzy ends that were probably the result of over-bleaching. Dark circles rimmed her eyes. She waved them into the apartment impatiently. The air inside smelled of stale cigarette smoke and closed-up rooms. Deep shadows shrouded the corners of the living room, and all the shades were drawn. Kate hung back near the door as Jim and Alice took the lead.

Jim offered the woman his most charming smile. "We appreciate your call, Miss …?"

If she was charmed, her frown was a good way to hide it. "Misty Rayne."

"Misty Rayne?" Alice asked, her voice tinged with incredulity. "Pretty name."

The young woman shrugged. "That's my stage name. I'm taking modeling classes when I'm not waiting tables. You said you're looking for John MacFarlane. He hasn't won a sweepstakes or come into money from a long-lost relative, has he?"

Jim shook his head. "No, we just need him to sign a paper."

"Good." Misty crossed the room and picked up a pack of cigarettes. "I hope they're lawsuit papers. I'd hate to help him get anything good."

"Apparently you're not the only one who feels that way," Jim said. "He's missing, and it looks like he didn't go willingly."

The woman blew out a puff of smoke and smiled for the first time. "You've made my day. I'm afraid I don't know where John is."

"Can you tell us what you do know?" Alice asked.

After another puff of smoke, Misty stubbed out the cigarette on a saucer that was clearly doubling as an ashtray. "I know he promised to marry me about a month ago. He promised me a nice place to live. I believed him too. I even believed I was in love. He can be very charming."

"I know."

The tone of Alice's answer made Misty look at her sharply, then harrumph. "We should form a support group. Anyway, I dumped him when I found out he'd made the same promise to two other women, and I haven't talked to him since then." She shook her head. "I should have known he was a scammer when he turned out to be into all that 'positive affirmation' junk. Anyone who spends that much time telling himself how great he is ..." Her voice trailed off and she looked wistfully at the pack of cigarettes.

"You can smoke if you need to," Alice said.

The woman shook her head. "I'm trying to quit. It's hard."

Jim nodded. "I remember. It's worth it though."

She shrugged. "Maybe. I can certainly use the money I spend on those things. Besides, my kid wants me to." She nodded toward a small framed photo that stood on a television stand in the room. Kate took a step closer to the photo to look. In it, Misty was smiling, with none of the shadows that were in her face now. Beside her, a little girl with a round face and deep dimples grinned at the camera.

"She's adorable," Kate said. "How old is she?"

"She's five. That photo's recent." Misty cast another glance at the cigarettes and sighed. "They showed her some scary pictures of lungs at school. Now she checks to see if I'm still breathing every time I fall asleep. I figured I should quit before the kid worries herself to death."

"Sounds like she loves you," Alice said gently.

Misty's face softened. "Yeah. She's a great kid. She's out Christmas shopping with her grandmother right now." She sighed. "With my work hours, she spends more time with my mom than she does with me."

"Do you know the names of the other women in John's life?" Alice asked.

She shrugged. "I know two. One works with me at Slammin', but I don't think she knows anything. She figured out what he was even before I did. Now she's dating one of the bartenders, a real nice guy."

"And the other woman?"

Misty smiled grimly. "She doesn't work at the club, but she's connected. If John's disappearance is because of her … well, he might not ever reappear."

"Why do you say that?" Jim asked.

"Because she's a very scary woman," Misty said. "And her brother is just as scary."

Jim crossed his arms over his chest. "And her name?"

"Elina Vasin. Her brother owns the club. She's crazy, I think. I've only met her a couple of times, but it's like looking at a cobra, you know? Cold and spooky. Anyway, Serge is very protective of his sister. I think if he found out about the romance and how John cheated on all of us, it wouldn't go well for him. Not that *I'd* tell Serge."

"I heard your boss has ties to organized crime," Kate said, stepping closer to the group.

The woman glanced at the cigarettes again and then twisted her fingers together as if to lock them before they could grab for the package. "I don't know anything about my boss's ties. I make it a point *not* to know things like that. I go to work every night, and I collect my paychecks. That's all I want to know about it. I have a kid, and talking about the boss isn't healthy."

"I can understand that," Alice said.

"I can tell you one thing. If Serge did go after John, someone ought to give him a medal. The world will be a better place with one less cheating creep in it."

"I think we need to go back over to the club when it opens," Jim said as they walked back to the car. "So far, all the clues we have circle back there."

Kate felt a jolt of nerves. "Do you mind if I don't go with you?"

Alice squeezed her arm. "Of course we don't mind. We'll let you know whatever we find." They reached the car and Alice looked over at Jim. "The club won't be open for hours. How do we spend the time in the meanwhile?"

"How about lunch?" Jim asked.

"After all that breakfast you ate?"

He shrugged. "All of us manly men are big eaters."

"I wouldn't mind some lunch," Kate admitted. "My stomach would appreciate something that isn't sugar and coffee."

They found a diner close by with food that was fortunately better than its decor. Jim had insisted on the place, even though the building looked suspiciously like it was once a battered mobile home and the parking lot sported an impressive collection of weeds sprouting between the cracks in the pavement.

"We'll go inside," Alice said. "But I'm not committing until I see what their health code status is."

"Coward," Jim said. "This is the kind of place I look for when I'm traveling. This is where you really get a feeling for the local cuisine."

"As long as that feeling isn't gastrointestinal distress," Alice said.

Tinsel garlands draped the walls inside the small diner. Above the cashier's stand, a mounted deer head was festive with a bright red clown nose and lights woven through the antlers. Below the deer's head, the diner proudly displayed its surprisingly good health code status.

"See?" Jim said. "O ye of little faith."

"Fine, but I'm not forgetting that place you took me to in Alabama."

Jim just tutted as they walked to their table. "Every restaurant has an off day." Throughout the small dining area, each table had candy cane–striped napkin holders, snowman-shaped condiment dispensers, and little bobblehead figurines.

After she finished a sloppy but delicious sandwich, Kate pushed her plate away before the chips on it could tempt her. "That was better than I expected."

"Places like this are the hidden gems of the road," Jim said as he grabbed one of Kate's rejected chips.

"Is that right?" Kate asked as she tapped the bobblehead Santa on the noggin. The little figure nodded with enthusiasm. "He certainly agrees with you."

"He's just trying to get on our good side," Alice said. "So we'll rescue him from this place."

"I can't take him away from his bobblehead friends," Kate said, gesturing toward the other tables where bobbing snowmen, reindeer, and Santas all smiled overly cheerful smiles.

"You're always so kindhearted," Alice teased. Then she turned to Jim. "What do we do next?"

"As long as we're already in Fort Worth, I'd like to go back to your ex's apartment," Jim said. "We can't be certain he'd call us. I want to ask his neighbor if he came home."

They agreed and made the drive to the classier area where John lived.

When they arrived, police cars with lights flashing greeted the trio ominously. They exchanged worried looks as they stepped from the Mustang. As soon as they walked into the building, they saw uniformed officers milling around John's apartment door. One of the officers stepped forward to stand in their way. "Can I help you?"

"I'm looking for John MacFarlane," Alice said, peering over the officer's shoulder. "That's his apartment. Is something wrong?"

"How do you know Mr. MacFarlane?" the officer asked as he pulled a pad of paper from his shirt pocket.

"I was married to him."

The officer looked startled and then turned to one of the other men behind him. "Get Matthews."

"Matthews?" Kate echoed. "*Peter* Matthews?"

The officer turned back to her. "How do you know Detective Matthews?"

"You're just full of questions today," Jim drawled, "but not many answers. Maybe we'll just wait for the detective."

Peter walked briskly out of John's apartment. His hair

was even wilder than usual, the result of the nervous habit of running his fingers through it. Kate could always tell how much a case was stressing Peter by the state of his hair. Clearly this one was very upsetting.

He nodded at the officer. "I've got this."

"What is a homicide detective doing at John's apartment?" Alice asked. Her voice sounded strained, and Kate looked quickly at her friend. Alice's face had gone pale.

"I'm sorry," Peter said, a slight frown creasing his forehead. His voice was gentle. "We got a tip last night that a body with a gunshot wound had washed up on the banks of Eagle Mountain Lake. That's what the call I got at your house was about," he added, nodding at Kate. "The tip was pretty nonspecific on location, so it took us most of the night to find him. Technically, I don't join the hunt until a body turns up, but I had a bad feeling about this one." He paused, then spoke even more quietly. "It was him."

Though she must have expected the news, Alice gasped and grew even more pale. She looked at Jim, her face a mask of misery. She started to speak but then just shook her head. Jim quickly wrapped his arms around her. "What happened?" he asked Peter.

"We won't know for sure until the coroner's report," Peter said. "But from the angle of the gunshot wound to his chest, it wasn't suicide. It looks like your husband was murdered."

Seven

The air in the hallway around them seemed electric for a moment. Kate couldn't believe it. She had never liked John MacFarlane, but she had met him. He was a real person, someone she knew. In a way, it was like the death of her book publisher all over again. *Normal people go through their whole lives without knowing any murdered people. What does that say about me?*

Then she processed exactly what Peter had said and corrected him. "John was Alice's *ex*-husband."

"That's not what I heard at your house," Peter said. He turned to Alice. "Isn't that the whole reason you're both here, because he technically *wasn't* your *ex*-husband?"

"I suppose it is," Alice said, her voice flat. "Though he certainly *felt* like an ex-husband. I can't believe he's dead. For years when we were married, I worried because of the crazy schemes he came up with. I constantly waited for someone to show up at the door and say what you've just said, but it's still a shock somehow. I guess when we found out he was missing, I assumed he'd show up with some crazy lie to explain why he'd missed our meeting and why it wasn't his fault."

Peter looked at her apologetically. "I hate to ask this, but I'm going to need you two to come down to the station and answer some questions."

Kate put an arm around Alice and turned to face Peter, frowning. "You can't think they did anything wrong."

Peter looked at her. "I wouldn't be doing my job if I didn't take them down for questions. They came to Fort Worth specifically to find him. And I stood right in your house and heard Jim threaten to kill the man."

"That's just something people say," Kate said.

"Including convicted murderers."

Building frustration raised Kate's voice. "You know he didn't mean it."

Jim reached out and put a hand on Kate's arm. "It's OK. Peter's doing his job. We understand." He turned to look at Peter. "Does Kate need to come with us? You *know* she's not involved with John's death. She only met the man briefly years ago."

Peter shook his head and looked at Kate. "I'll have a uniformed officer drive you home."

"I don't want to just leave you both," Kate said, reaching out to grip Alice's hand in support.

Alice gave her an encouraging smile. "Jim didn't kill anyone, so we don't have to worry. We'll call you as soon as we're done answering questions. You should go home."

Peter took a step toward Kate, clearly intending to say something, but she backed up. "I'll wait outside for my ride." She turned and hurried outside. It wouldn't help Jim and Alice if she started yelling at Peter. She knew that. She still didn't appreciate his manner.

She paced back and forth on the sidewalk in front of the apartment. She didn't like Peter thinking he needed to look after her any more than she liked him hauling her friends off for questioning. She thought of all the times her own ex-husband had told her what to do. Harry always just assumed she'd obey as well. And she did. She *always* did. But she wasn't that girl anymore.

Kate pulled out her phone and called Vivi. Her friend

greeted her cheerfully, and Kate told her about her situation. Vivi listened without interruption before asking, "Do you want me to come get you?"

"Only if you can spare the time and it won't get you in trouble at work."

"Where are you?"

Kate gave her the address, and Vivi said she knew where it was.

"That's not far. I'll come get you, but you'll have to come back to the hotel with me for a while. I can't make the run to Sage Hills right now. I only have a couple more hours of work if you don't mind hanging out here." Kate agreed and walked to the entrance of the apartment complex to wait for Vivi.

The breeze was chilly and Kate pulled her thick crochet jacket close around her. She turned her face toward the sun and closed her eyes as the warmth bathed her face. In Maine, the winter sun sometimes seemed to carry no warmth at all, but it was different in Texas. She could barely believe Christmas was so close. They'd already had their first and second snows back in Stony Point. Kate didn't miss shoveling, and she didn't miss feeling half-frozen all the time. Still, Stony Point would look like a Christmas card by now. Texas sure didn't.

"Miss?" Kate turned to see a uniformed officer trot up. His face was pink from running, and his expression distraught. "Are you Miss Stevens?"

Kate nodded.

"I'm supposed to drive you home."

"I have my own ride."

The young officer shifted his feet. "The detective said I was supposed to drive you home."

"I understand that the detective might be your superior, but he is not mine. I have my own ride. If he wants to speak with me about it, he can call when he's done harassing my friends."

The young officer swallowed hard, and his Adam's apple bobbed. "I'd really rather not tell him that," he said.

Kate felt a pang of guilt for upsetting someone who hadn't done anything to her. "Just tell him that I got a ride with a friend." Vivi's blue Mini Cooper pulled up, and her friend waved. "That's her now. Thank you for your offer, officer."

As they drove away, Vivi glanced into her rearview mirror. "What did you do to that police officer? He looked terrified."

"Peter ordered him to take me home. I wouldn't go."

"Ah, that would do it."

As they headed back to the hotel, Kate caught Vivi up in more detail about everything she'd done since she's seen Vivi last. She ended with the confrontation at the apartment. "Sure, Jim said he'd kill John if he didn't sign the paper, but he didn't mean it. Honestly, I might have said those very words about my ex once or twice."

"From the sound of it, the guy was already dead when Jim threatened him."

Kate blinked at her friend. "You think?"

"It has to be. You told me that Peter was called away from your tree decorating when there were reports of a dead body at Eagle Mountain Lake. That body turned out to be John. That means John was already dead when Jim made his remark."

"Right," Kate agreed. "And he'd have to be stupid to say something like that after he'd killed someone."

"Plus, they probably weren't even in Fort Worth yet when the guy died," Vivi suggested.

Kate shook her head. "I remember Jim telling me they'd arrived a day before they came to see me. No luck there."

"And it will be complicated if and when the police discover y'all were in John's apartment the same night his body was found." Vivi flashed a smile at her friend. "I'm sure it'll all work out. Still, we have a decision to make."

"What's that?"

"Alice and Jim are probably going to be answering questions for a long time," Vivi said. "So, the big question is, do you just want to go home when I get off work, or should we do some investigating of our own? We could follow up on the dance club."

"You can't be suggesting that we go to that club. I thought you were as scared of Serge Vasin as I am."

Vivi shrugged. "The club sounds exciting. We can grab some supper in the city and then go see what we can find out. If we're careful, I'm sure we'll be fine."

Kate looked down at her jeans and the crochet jacket she was wearing over a long-sleeved T-shirt. "I'm not exactly dressed to go clubbing."

"So, we go back to Sage Hills after work, change, then hit the club."

"You're really serious?"

"We don't have to." Vivi finally relented, but Kate could hear the disappointment in her voice.

"Just give me a little while to process the idea."

Vivi did. When they reached the Hamilton Arms Hotel, Vivi showed Kate to her office. The room was far plainer than Kate had expected, without the plush carpets and vivid colors of the hotel's public areas. A single narrow window had white blinds that matched the office's white walls. A tiny desk and chair sat against the windowed wall. A printer stand, a file cabinet, a small bookcase with a hopeful-looking African violet, and a second floor-to-ceiling bookcase were the only other furniture. Though the furniture was spare, it still almost filled the small room.

Kate pointed to the potted plant. "You must be getting over your black thumb."

Vivi shook her head. "I just got it yesterday." She cupped her hands over the small plant and whispered, "The poor thing doesn't know its days are numbered."

Kate laughed and looked around for something else positive to say. "Well, your office is cozy."

"You mean small. I don't spend much time in here except for when I need some privacy," Vivi said. "Now I have to run and check on preparations for a huge holiday party." She shook her head. "It's for an environmental business organization with a huge membership. Lots of companies are going to be here for it, and I'm knee-deep in details."

"Is there a strong environmental movement in Texas?" Kate asked. "I guess I pictured Texas being more cigars and beef cattle."

"Envirotech in Texas is big business," Vivi said as she gathered up a clipboard stuffed with papers. "The public is getting pickier about what companies do to our state. Look, I'll be back as quick as I can. Will you be OK?"

Kate nodded. "Can I use your computer?"

"Sure, have fun."

Kate settled down at Vivi's desk and surfed fashion sites. She did that whenever she had time. She got inspiration from the ways other designers used unusual fabrics or trims or colors. She often found herself picturing ways to get a similar look with crochet. She pulled a notebook from her purse to take notes on any new ideas that came to her. As soon as the holidays were over, she had a new book to work on.

Time passed surprisingly quickly, as it always did when Kate gave herself over to crochet or even thinking about crochet. Her art was one of the great joys of her life. Maybe Jim was right. She needed to focus on the good things in front of her and stop moping about not getting exactly what she wanted.

When Vivi returned, Kate glanced at the computer and was surprised to see how late it had gotten. "I'm ready to go," Vivi said. "I'm sorry I never got back in here. I hope you weren't bored out of your mind."

"Not a bit." Kate closed her notebook. "I spent the time brainstorming some new crochet designs. Now I'm practically itching to get yarn in my hands."

"Are you trying to back out of going to the club?"

Kate shook her head. "No. I think we have to find out as much as we can about who really killed John so that Peter loses interest in Jim and Alice."

"I doubt he *really* suspects either of them," Vivi said. "He just has to follow procedure. It's his job."

Kate nodded. "I suppose, but I'd just feel better if I could find someplace else for Peter to look."

"Then let's go clubbing."

Going clubbing didn't turn out to be quite that simple. On the drive back to Sage Hills, Kate admitted that she didn't have a single thing that would be appropriate for club wear.

"I have a few things," Vivi said. "You'd be amazed at the wardrobe you build up in my job. I could loan you something."

Kate smiled at her friend. "I don't think we're the same size. I'm not exactly tall, but you're *tiny*."

"That's the thing about club clothes," Vivi said. "If a dress is a little small, that only makes it more perfect."

Kate moaned. She had a feeling that she was going to seriously regret this decision.

Once they got to Vivi's house and her friend began holding scraps of slinky fabric up in front of her, Kate nearly whimpered. "Don't you have a dress with more *dress* in it?"

"Of course," Vivi said. "And they're all perfect for church. But we're going clubbing. You want to blend in, right?" She held up a black dress. "How about this one? It's the longest hem I have in club-style dresses."

"I could try it on, I guess," Kate answered, though the neckline seemed awfully low. She quickly slipped it on and discovered several things. She'd never been accused of being chesty, but the dress exposed most of what she had to view. Plus, it was the tightest dress she'd ever wiggled into, and the back slit in the skirt was disturbingly high. "I don't know. I don't think this is my size, and it's definitely not my style."

"You look gorgeous," Vivi said. "And you'll blend in. We'll slip in, get some information, and get out. Think of yourself as a secret agent."

Kate continued to look in the mirror in alarm. "I think James Bond wore a lot more clothes."

"Just keep in mind that everyone will be dressed like this," Vivi said. "So, you'll be less noticeable in that dress than in something of your own. Think of it like a bathing suit. You'd be embarrassed to wear a bathing suit out in public except when everyone on the beach is wearing the same kind of thing."

"I believe my bathing suit covers more," Kate said as she tugged the neckline up and the hem down.

She felt compelled to do something to help Jim and Alice, so she finally gave in. Vivi offered to drive to the club. Kate, meanwhile, spent the ride telling herself that everything would be all right.

When the bouncer at the door waved her in without the amused grin he'd offered last time, Kate had to admit she was clearly fitting in better. Once inside, the noise and crowd were just as overwhelming as on her last visit. "We need to stay together," she yelled over the music.

Vivi nodded, and Kate saw that her eyes sparkled with excitement at the whirl of activity around them. Kate was amazed at her friend. *We really couldn't be less alike,* she thought.

"Let's try the bar!" Vivi yelled back. "Bartenders know everything and everyone."

Kate let Vivi tow her through the crowd. She still found the crush and noise disorienting but realized that she felt less panicky. She clearly was never going to be a club girl, but at least she found she could breathe more easily.

The bar was far enough from the speakers that some talk was possible, as long as they didn't mind talking loudly. Vivi turned her elfin grin on the tall, handsome bartender, and he returned the smile as he leaned across the bar toward her. "What can I do for you?"

"I'm looking for John MacFarlane. Have you seen him?"

The bartender turned serious. "You don't want him. He's a bum."

Vivi nodded. "I know. He's a rat. You know him?"

The man nodded. "He comes in a lot. I haven't seen him tonight. You should stay away from him. My girlfriend was involved with him for a while before we started dating, and I'm still trying to convince her that all men aren't vermin."

"I heard he likes to make promises to lots of women," Kate said.

"If you know that, why do you want to see him?" the bartender asked.

Vivi shrugged. "Maybe I want to form a support group with the other spurned women. Are there many here? Could you point some out? Could we talk to your girlfriend?"

The bartender backed away from her. "No. I definitely don't need you stirring up memories of John MacFarlane with her."

"Then point us toward someone else he did wrong."

"I mind my own business." His eyes darted to the crowd behind them and widened. He quickly hurried to the other end of the bar. Kate turned to see what could have upset the bartender. She found herself looking directly into the ice-blue eyes of Serge Vasin.

Vasin's gaze swept from the toes of Kate's very high heels up to her face. Kate felt a blush burning behind her skin as Vasin smiled at her. "You have learned the dress code, but I think I liked you better before. You are more of a shy wild rose than a showy orchid."

As Kate stammered for a response, Vasin's gaze turned to Vivi. "You are a friend to Kate?"

Vivi raised her chin. "I am. We're trying to find out about John MacFarlane."

The man sighed. "Surely a waste of time for two such beautiful women. You should be dancing and enjoying the night."

"Maybe after we get a few answers," Vivi said. She added a smile. "I do like dancing."

Vasin's eyes never strayed long from Kate, and she fought the urge to fidget under the intensity of his gaze. "Your sister could help us," Kate suggested hesitantly. "We understand she was seeing John for a while."

Vasin smiled grimly at that. "My sister's choices are her own. I do not get involved. I would suggest you do not ask her about him. She has a quick temper, and she does not enjoy being reminded of her mistakes."

"How about you?" Kate asked. "Do you have a quick temper?"

"Not with beautiful women, even if they do ask foolish questions."

"But with men?" Kate asked. "Especially men who've hurt your sister?"

Vasin laughed, a quick bark of sound. "My sister does not need me to fight her battles. If I tried to do so, she would quickly show me the error of my ways." He shook his head. "I do not get involved in Elina's love life."

"You said Elina has a temper," Vivi said. "Do you think she might hurt John?"

"I think you should ask her," Vasin said. "Or perhaps not. As I said, she has a temper, and you do not want it directed at you." He took a step closer, crowding Kate's personal space. "Would you like to come and sit at my table? I can buy you a drink and we can talk about more pleasant things."

"No, thank you," Kate said, edging back away from him. "We really do need to find someone who will talk to us about John. I need to know what kind of trouble he was in."

"Was?" Vasin asked. "Is he no longer in trouble?"

"He's no longer much of anything," Kate answered as she took another step back. "The police found his body. He was murdered."

"That is too bad."

"Really?" Kate asked.

The man's face looked even more amused. "You think I killed him? You have such an unfortunate opinion of me."

"I don't have any opinion at all," Kate answered. "I don't know you."

"Then come back to my table. We can get to know each other, and you can form an opinion."

"I'm seeing someone," Kate stammered, taking another step back. She caught a glance of Vivi from the corner of her eye. Her friend clearly didn't know quite what to do.

Vasin's smile grew wider. "Lucky man, but foolish, I think. He lets you come to my club alone? This is not a wise choice for a man who wants to keep his woman."

Kate froze, suddenly angry. "He's my friend, not my keeper."

Vasin burst into laughter, which made Kate even angrier. She stomped one foot and sent him into more peals of laughter. Kate stepped to one side, intending to stomp away, but Vasin caught her arm.

"Hey!" Vivi said, tugging on Vasin's sleeve. "Hands off."

He let go of Kate and held up his hands. "I mean your friend no harm." Then the smile slid from his face, and he looked at her seriously. "Please, dance and enjoy the club, but be careful, little tigers. Some here have far bigger teeth than you. I would not like to see you hurt."

Kate felt an icy whisper of fear. She didn't know if Vasin was warning them or threatening them, but she suddenly felt the urge to run away—very far and very fast."

Eight

Though Kate had resisted the urge to run screaming from the club, she and Vivi didn't stay much longer. No one they spoke to seemed interested in talking about John MacFarlane or Elina Vasin.

Kate spotted Misty Rayne passing through the crowd with a tray and headed toward the young woman. Misty spotted her and her eyes widened in panic. She shook her head once. Kate nodded and let the young woman pass.

Vivi leaned close. "Who was that?"

"One of John's conquests," Kate said into Vivi's ear. "She already spoke to us, but now she seems scared."

"I bet she's scared of her boss," Vivi said.

Kate nodded. Vasin certainly scared *her*.

More than one person looked around uneasily as soon as they started asking questions, and Kate caught Vasin's bouncer following them. By the time the music began to make Kate's head ache, they realized they weren't going to learn anything else.

When she got home, Kate took something for her headache and tumbled into bed. She woke to a room flooded with morning sunshine and the sound of the telephone. She glanced at her clock and yelped. She'd overslept by hours. She scrambled to her purse and pulled out her phone without glancing at the ID. "Hello?"

"Hi, Kate. We're finally sprung."

Kate recognized Alice's voice. "Oh, I'm so glad. Please tell me you weren't there all night."

"It felt like it," Alice said. "It was late when they let us go, and I didn't want to wake you. I'm still not sure Jim is totally in the clear. Your friend was very cordial, but he had a lot of questions that we had to answer over and over. Then he made it clear he doesn't want us leaving Texas until he finds John's killer."

"How are you doing?" Kate asked gently. "I know John put you through a lot, but it's still got to be hard to hear he was murdered."

"I'm trying not to think too much about that part," Alice said softly. Then she cleared her throat. "Jim and I are going to come straight over, if that's OK with you. We can talk about our next move together. I'm still thinking Jim and I should go to the club tonight."

"About that. Um ... I went last night with Vivi."

Alice's voice was shocked. "You did? I thought you were scared to death of that place."

"I wanted to help. I guess I felt guilty about Peter taking you both in for questioning. Besides, it seemed like a good idea to go back to the club before the police got there to ask their own questions about John. People are only going to get more resistant to talking with the police involved."

"Did you learn anything?" Alice asked.

"I spoke to Serge Vasin," Kate said. "He seemed surprised that John was dead, but I don't know how much of that could have been put-on. He's a scary guy. He also said his sister has a dangerous temper and would fight her own battles."

"That's interesting," Alice said. "So maybe we need to talk to the sister."

"Are you sure? I mean, the whole reason you came to Texas was so you could marry Jim. With John gone, isn't that problem settled? Maybe it's something for the police to handle now?"

"Jim and I talked about that. I didn't like John. I haven't liked him for a long time, but he was my husband a long time ago. Somehow it feels like that should matter, like I should do something to help find his killer. Plus, I'm not sure I'll feel free and clear as long as the police are looking at Jim and me as potential suspects."

"I can understand that," Kate agreed.

"So, are we good to come over? You don't have to be involved if you'd rather not. It sounded like Peter wouldn't like it."

"Peter doesn't control me," Kate answered with more heat than she intended.

"I heard *that*. Jim and I are on the way."

Kate tossed the phone back into her purse and then headed for the bedroom to change and make her bed. As she pulled on a pair of dark knit slacks and a chunky crochet sweater in shades of burgundy and forest green, she wondered what they should do next. She was brushing her shoulder-length brown hair when she heard the knock on the door.

As she pulled the door open, she said, "You must have reached warp speed to get here that fast." Then she stopped when she realized it wasn't Jim and Alice in the doorway. It was Peter. She straightened and frowned at him. "Oh."

Peter smiled ruefully. "Still not in my fan club, I see. May I come in?"

"It depends," she said, folding her arms over her chest. "Did you come with more orders you expect me to follow?"

"You pick the oddest times to get stubborn. I'm just trying to keep you safe."

"I can get along just fine without you."

Peter blinked at her. "Is that what you want? To be without me?"

The hurt on Peter's face made Kate's posture soften. "No. Surely we can find some middle ground."

"I'd be willing to try."

Kate stepped out of the doorway to let Peter in. "I assume Alice and Jim told you everything we've done so far to look for John."

"I can't talk about an active investigation," he said.

"Fine, but there's something they didn't know. I'm going to tell you, but you cannot rant at me until I tell you the whole thing. Got it?"

He nodded, his mouth drawn into a straight, flat line of unhappiness.

"I went back to Slammin' last night to see if anyone knew what kind of trouble John might be in." She saw Peter flinch and open his mouth, and she held up a hand. "No ranting until I'm done, remember?"

His mouth snapped closed and he nodded, so she went on. "No one was willing to speak with us except Serge Vasin." She noticed Peter's eyes were looking a little buggy, but she continued. "He didn't deny that his sister had been seeing John. He didn't offer much information, but he said he wouldn't have gotten involved with his sister's love life and that she could handle it herself. I'm betting she knew John was cheating on her, and she comes from a scary family. You might want to talk to her."

Peter waited a moment after she finished talking. Then he spoke very calmly. "Are you done?"

She nodded.

"Serge Vasin is a very bad man. I want you to—" He paused. "I *highly recommend* that you stay as far away from him as possible. I recommend that you stay away from this whole investigation. I'll find out who killed MacFarlane. I don't need help."

"I'm not certain Alice and Jim can let it go," Kate said. "And if they can't, I can't. They're my friends. But I promise to keep you updated on what I do."

"I'm not sure that's much of a compromise." He pointed at her. "You do know it's against the law to interfere with an active investigation, so this isn't just me being controlling."

"We won't interfere," Kate said, smiling sweetly. "We'll *assist*."

Peter groaned. "At least stay away from Vasin. He's not a nice guy. As much as it pains me to say it, if you must keep on with this, stay close to Jim. I get the impression he can take care of himself."

"And I can't?"

"Please, Kate, you're hurting me here. I just want you to stay safe."

Kate crossed her arms again. "I won't intentionally put myself in danger." She watched the play of emotion on his face; then she asked, "Do you want a cup of coffee?"

"I can't. I have to get to the office. Are you sure you've told me everything?"

"Well, there was a phone call."

Peter looked at her expectantly.

"Someone called the other night and just said curiosity killed the cat. Vivi thought it might be a teen prank since the kids are off from school. You know, the modern equivalent of 'Is your refrigerator running?' or 'Do you have Prince Albert in a can?'"

He nodded. "Maybe. This neighborhood is outside my jurisdiction, but I have friends at Sage Hills PD. I'll see if I can get an extra drive-by for your house at night."

"Thank you."

He sighed deeply. "I really do have to go. This is supposed to be my nap break after being up all night, but I have to get back now. You be careful."

"I will."

He nodded and then kissed her cheek and left. Kate curled up on the love seat and began working on Vanessa's Christmas sweater. The steady movement of the hook and the yarn through her fingers was relaxing, freeing her mind to think as she worked on the intricate, lacy design.

She didn't enjoy frustrating Peter, but she still remembered how easy it had been to turn herself over to Harry when they were married. He was only happy when she did exactly what he wanted. Since she wanted to keep the peace, Kate spent years feeling like a robot following someone else's commands. She'd lost herself. She wasn't going to let that happen again.

She was surprised at how much of the sweater she'd finished by the time a knock came at the door. She hurried to let Alice and Jim in. They both looked tired, though they were in fresh clothes. Jim's hair was still damp from the shower he'd taken just before they left the hotel. Kate quickly hugged them both. "Was it awful?"

"Not the worst I've ever experienced," Jim said dryly. "Your boyfriend didn't break out the rubber hoses or dunk us in water."

Kate's eyes widened in horror. "Someone's done that to you before?"

Jim looked at her solemnly for a moment; then a smile tugged at the corner of his mouth. "No. I did have an unpleasant talk with an army officer in Rwanda once, but it didn't progress much past poking me in the chest and bellowing threats. At least Peter doesn't bellow."

"No, but he's not happy that I won't promise to stay out of the investigation," Kate said.

"Speaking of not being happy," Jim said, "I had a half-dozen voice mails on my phone when they gave it back.

Apparently, Misty Rayne wants to make it very clear that she doesn't know us, especially when she's at work. Something definitely has that young woman spooked."

"She did look pretty upset when she saw me at the club last night," Kate said. "When she thought I was going to talk to her, she practically panicked."

"So *you're* the one who worked her up," Jim said.

"Not intentionally."

"Don't feel bad. If we're not stirring up trouble, we're just not having fun," Alice said cheerfully.

"Do you think Misty reacted like she did because of the murder?" Kate asked. "Could she be more involved than she pretended?"

"Hard to say," Jim answered. "She might simply be afraid of the Vasins. She did point us toward the crazy sister, and she could be regretting that. Or she might be afraid of losing her job by talking out of turn."

"Either way, we should leave the poor woman alone. She has a little girl, and I don't want to be responsible for her getting fired—or worse," Alice said. "Let's go over the clues we have. We know John was lying to a number of women."

"Including the scary sister of a possible crime boss," Kate said.

"Including her," Alice said. "So, that could be the trouble he was in, but it doesn't explain the file folder under his mattress."

"Also we have a flash drive, but we don't know what's on it," Jim added. "It could simply be another copy of the photos from the folder. Though with a guy like John, he could have compromising photos of someone's wife. I doubt he was above blackmail."

"No, he wasn't," Alice agreed. "And that brings us back to the photos. John doesn't collect things unless he has an angle. What could be the angle in a bunch of photos at a work site? The men aren't burying a body or cooking drugs. There's nothing to the photos that looks incriminating."

"Can I ask a question?" Kate asked. "How is it that you still have the photos? Didn't you give them to Peter?"

"We didn't have them with us," Jim admitted. "But we do now."

Alice pulled the file from her oversized purse. "We want to turn the file over to Peter as soon as possible. We don't want to look like we're withholding evidence. But maybe we could scan the photos first? Is there a place around here where we can do that?"

"My studio," Kate said. "I have a good scanner since I have to be able to scan things for my books." She led them into the studio, and they set to work sending the scans to Kate's laptop. While they were working, Jim used Kate's big magnifying glass to look over the photos.

"I wish we could see more of this logo," he said.

Kate looked through the glass. "I need to show that to Vivi. She might recognize it. And Peter might, as well."

"Right, right," Jim agreed. "We'll hand them over to Peter soon. Maybe along the way we could pay a visit to Elina Vasin. I'd like to see if she's as intimidating as her reputation suggests."

Kate had more or less promised Peter not to go see Serge Vasin, but she hadn't made any promises about the sister, so she quickly agreed to go with them. Again they piled into Alice's car and drove into Fort Worth.

"How do you know where she lives?" Kate asked.

"Apparently the Vasin siblings are practically celebrities here, and celebrities don't get much privacy," Alice said. "Elina's apartment was included in some huge puff piece about interior design in Fort Worth. I found the article online and it gave us all the details we need."

They pulled up outside the fancy apartment house and handed over the convertible keys to the valet attendant. "And I thought John was living well," Alice said. "This place makes his apartment building look like a hovel."

They walked into the lobby and quickly found that actually getting to Elina's apartment was going to be difficult. A man with a shaved head and a dark suit stood beside the elevators. When they walked toward the elevator doors, the man stepped forward. "Who are you here to see?"

"Elina Vasin," Alice said.

"She's not expecting you." There was no question in his voice.

"No, not unless she's psychic," Jim answered in his easy drawl. "But we'd still like to talk to her."

"That won't be possible."

"I might have to insist," Jim said.

The man actually smiled at that. He eased open his jacket to reveal a holstered gun. "You all should leave."

Kate felt a jolt of alarm as Jim rolled his shoulders and stood eye to eye with the armed man. "What if we're not ready to do that?"

The tension in the lobby ramped up a notch as both men stood ramrod stiff, and Kate suddenly wondered if she should have followed Peter's directions after all.

Nine

Alice eased Jim back and gave the other man a sweet smile. "Could you possibly tell Miss Vasin that we'd like to talk with her about John MacFarlane? She might be happy to talk to us. We belong to the same club."

The man's gaze never moved from Jim as he asked, "What club?"

"The John MacFarlane anti-fan club," Alice said.

The man's eyes finally shifted to her. "I can pass along a message, but you're not leaving this lobby until I hear back."

"Fine," Jim said. "We weren't looking to go anywhere."

They backed away as the man spoke on a cellphone. Alice gave Jim a look. "Try not to get us shot today."

"I've dealt with his kind before, especially when I was taking combat photos. He wasn't going to shoot anyone," Jim said. "He just wanted to be sure we knew he was tough."

"Isn't that what you were trying to prove too?" Alice asked.

Jim grinned wickedly. "Sweetheart, I *am* tough."

The elevator guard stepped closer and spoke in a flat, serious tone. "Miss Vasin will see you. Good luck." He waved them toward the elevator.

"Good luck? Why do I suddenly wish we hadn't gotten our way?" Kate asked.

When the elevator's doors opened again, they faced a hallway with butter-colored walls and a plush carpet. A set of beautiful, ornate doors stood open, and a thin woman with an equally thin smile stood in the doorway. She was dressed in a black pantsuit with a silver belt. Her nail polish shone blood-red as did her lipstick. She surveyed the trio with a frigidity that made Kate shudder.

"I am Elina Vasin," she said. "You wanted to talk about John MacFarlane? I hope you aren't looking for praise for him. I have none to give."

"No," Alice said, looking at the woman levelly. "No one who knew John would look for that."

"Knew?" Elina echoed.

"John is dead," Jim said as he stepped up to stand beside Alice. "Murdered, apparently. He was shot in the chest."

The thin smile grew slightly. "And I thought this would not be a day for good news. Would you like to come in?"

"Thank you," Alice said.

They followed Elina through the doors and into an equally lush apartment filled with antiques and art. Elina waved them toward a sitting area. "You know who I am. Who are you?"

"I'm Alice MacFarlane," Alice said. "I was married to John at one time. This is my fiancé, Jim Parker, and my dear friend, Kate Stevens."

The woman nodded as she seemed to fold herself like origami and tucked herself into a beautiful Louis XVI chair. Then she turned and looked at Kate appraisingly. "It is good to have friends. I believe you have met my brother, Serge?"

Kate looked at her, shocked. "How did you know?"

"You fit the description of the Kate he met," Elina said. "He said you were a tiger who looked like a deer."

Kate felt the warmth of a blush. "I'm surprised he'd remark on me at all."

"You are unusual among the women Serge meets," Elina said. "He likes things that are unusual. But you have not come to talk about my brother. You wanted to discuss John MacFarlane. Would you like some refreshments as we talk?"

"No, thank you," Alice said. "We don't really intend to stay that long. We've heard you were involved with John."

"I was. He was handsome and charming, and I enjoy spending time with handsome, charming men. Then I learned I was not alone. I do not wish to be part of a harem, so I stopped being involved with him."

Jim leaned forward with both hands resting on the head of his cane. "You don't sound particularly heartbroken."

"My heart was not involved. And there are many handsome and charming men."

"Still, you must have been angry," Jim said.

"I was annoyed. I do not like to be made to look like a fool."

"How annoyed were you?"

She looked at him through half-closed eyes for a long moment and then turned to face Alice. "Your fiancé is nothing like John MacFarlane. Did your tastes change so much?"

"I grew up," Alice said. "And grew smarter."

"And yet *I* was involved with John," the woman said, her lids half closed again and her head dipped now as she spoke. "Am I immature or stupid?"

Alice didn't seem fazed by the subtle threat in the woman's voice. "You were smart enough to catch on to what John was, and you never married him. So, obviously, you were both more mature and smarter than I."

"Ah, that is a good answer. As anyone would tell you, it wouldn't be a good idea to think of me as stupid."

"And I wouldn't," Alice said. "I wasn't calling you names."

"If we were name-calling, we wouldn't choose 'stupid,'" Jim added. "'Formidable,' maybe."

This made Elina smile, though she kept her gaze entirely

on Alice. "I approve of this man you have chosen. What do you want to know?"

"I'd like to know who killed John."

Clearly startled, Elina laughed. "And you think I know?"

"We thought you might," Alice said.

"It is true that I can be a cold and vindictive woman. I am not averse to violence. I am very glad that John MacFarlane is dead. But if I had killed him, I would have left the body in such a way that it was clear that a cold and vindictive woman had become very angry with him."

"Really?" Jim said. "Wouldn't that bring the police right to your door? It seems like you'd be more subtle."

She laughed. "I am not afraid of the police, and I am not subtle. Serge is subtle." She shrugged, lifting one elegant shoulder. "As I said, if I had killed John, I would have made it clear that he annoyed me. I would have made it clear to him as well. Can you picture what I mean?"

Kate shuddered as her imagination went to an uncomfortably graphic place.

"I believe I can," Alice said calmly.

"And did John die in any of those ways?" Elina asked.

Alice shook her head. "The police haven't shared a lot of details, but he was shot once in the chest."

Elina smiled. "A waste of potential."

Alice visibly shuddered at that. "Do you have any idea who might have wanted John dead besides you?"

She shrugged again. "He apparently knew many women. If one of them lost her heart to him, she might be more than annoyed to find him a cheating pig."

"I don't suppose you'd make us a list?" Jim asked.

She smiled. "No. Though if you discover it was one of these women, tell her that I may pay her legal fees."

"Kind of you," Alice said.

Elina tilted her head almost in a nod. "I would make a different suggestion of who might have wanted to kill this man."

"Oh?" Jim said.

Elina didn't even glance his way but kept her eyes on Alice. "John told me he was going to be coming into a windfall. He boasted that he would be as wealthy as my brother. Such wealth is not always acquired legally, especially by a man like John. He was proud of this scheme, whatever it was, but would not give me any details. I asked. I do not like not knowing things. He would only give me one cryptic clue."

"Which was?" Alice asked.

"Green."

"Green, like money?" Alice asked.

Again Elina shrugged. "Perhaps. He did like money." The woman stood and crossed the room to a sideboard near the front door. Alice, Jim, and Kate stood. Elina plucked a business card from a beautiful celadon bowl and carried it to Alice. "If you find you need help while you search for this killer, call. I will do what I can. In exchange, I ask that you tell me what you learn when you are finished. As I said, I like to know things."

"I believe I can agree to that," Alice said, taking the card. "I appreciate your help."

Elina waved an elegant hand. "You brought me something different and diverting to think about. This is a gift. I thank you." Then she turned her icy blue gaze toward Kate. "If I were you, I would stay away from my brother."

Kate jumped a bit, startled. "Excuse me?" she whispered.

"I am not threatening you," Elina said, smiling. Her smile was not reassuring when matched with her cold blue eyes. "My brother also likes things that are different and diverting, but I think you would not like too much of his attention. Your life will not be improved by it. Serge is not like John MacFarlane, but he is still not a good man to love."

"Thank you for the advice," Kate stammered. "I'm not in danger of falling in love with your brother. I'm already involved with someone."

"This is good," Elina said. "But he is interested in you. That can be enough to make a problem sometimes. Take care, and do not let curiosity about my brother get you into trouble."

The remark about curiosity made Kate jump. "You called my house!"

Elina smiled, not even pretending to be shocked by the accusation. "I do not know what you are talking about. But if I were to speak with you at any time, I would only have your best interests at heart. Women have let curiosity lead them into trouble with my brother before. I would hate to see that happen."

Kate had no answer for that.

They said their goodbyes and Kate numbly followed her friends to the elevator. As soon as the elevator doors closed on them, Alice put an arm around Kate. "She freaked you out."

"I don't blame you," Jim added. "That's one intimidating woman."

"I'm sure she's the person who called my house." Kate explained about the phone call and Vivi's suggestion that it was just a prank. "But the wording was too close to what Elina said in there. Still, why would she call me? And how did she get my number? Do you think she's threatening me?"

"Threatening or warning, it's creepy either way," Alice said.

"I imagine a woman like Elina has all kinds of resources," Jim said. "Getting a cellphone number is probably not even a challenge. Still, I don't like it. I think we should try to keep some distance between us and the Vasins."

Kate shivered. "I can't imagine why John would get involved with her."

"The same reason John did anything," Alice said. "Money. Elina Vasin practically oozes money."

"Do you think Elina killed him?" Kate whispered.

Alice shook her head. "I suspect what she said was true. If she'd killed him, they'd have found him in bits or something equally horrifying. From what Peter told us, he was beaten up, but not all that badly. He would definitely have survived it."

"Did Peter give you any other clues?" Kate asked.

"Only what you already know. John was shot once at very close range and dumped in the lake." Alice paused and for a moment her face looked haunted. No matter what trouble they'd had, she had once been John's wife, and it was clear the murder was very upsetting for her. Finally, Alice seemed to shake off her thoughts, and she spoke in a more upbeat tone. "At least Jim doesn't have a gun and has never had a gun. That might be one of the things that got us out of the station, though I can't imagine it would be hard to get hold of a gun in a city."

"Especially a Texas city," Jim said.

When they got to the car, Alice handed a cellphone to Kate. "This is John's phone. Maybe the clue he gave Elina is also his password. Try out as many forms of the color green as you can think of. You're a designer, I know you can come up with a lot of names for green."

Kate settled into the backseat and brainstormed colors. She tried *green, hunter, turquoise, celadon, avocado, emerald,* and *jade*. None of them unlocked the phone. Then she tried *olive, sea, leaf,* and *malachite*. After that, she was stumped.

"Get anywhere?" Alice asked, glancing in the rearview mirror.

"No, sorry."

Alice nodded. "It was a long shot, but we should know by now that nothing ever turns out that easy." She glanced toward Jim. "So, where to now?"

"I'd like to see his apartment again," Jim said. "We might have missed something."

"Us *and* the police?" Alice asked. "That seems unlikely."

"We're a little stuck for leads," Jim answered. "So, revisiting is about all we have. Besides, I'd like to talk to his neighbor again and see if she knows anything about this 'green' windfall he was expecting."

At the apartment building, they started down the hall and found that the yellow crime scene tape was torn and hanging from the apartment door. Jim leaned close to look at the door lock and frame. "Whoever broke in didn't even bother to pick the lock," he said. "They just forced the door."

"We shouldn't go in there," Kate said. "Not with you two already under suspicion. I should call Peter and wait for him. Maybe you guys shouldn't even be here."

"He's not likely to imagine you got all the way here without your vehicle," Jim said. "No, we'll wait and stay out of the apartment. Even though I'm itching to see inside. Tell Peter we came to speak to John's neighbors; no reason to suggest we might have been willing to break into a crime scene."

Kate made the call, and they lurked in the hallway. They didn't have to wait long. Peter's stride alone told Kate that he wasn't thrilled to find her there. "Did any of you go inside?" he asked as he walked past them.

"No sir," Jim said.

"Good enough. Stay in the hall."

The apartment door was hanging open, so Peter led several uniformed officers in. Alice, Jim, and Kate edged close enough to see inside. The apartment looked as if a tornado had been through it. Everything smashable had been smashed. The upholstery on the sofa was slashed and wads of stuffing dotted the floor. "Someone was either very angry or looking for something," Jim whispered. "Or both."

"Whoever did that would have made a lot of noise," Alice said, backing away from the door. "So why didn't the neighbor call the police?"

"Excellent question." Jim turned and limped to the neighbor's door. He looked at it closely. "Someone forced this door too. Kate, get your boyfriend."

Jim pushed the door open with his toe to avoid smearing any possible fingerprints. He stood in the hall and called, "Miss? Are you all right? Miss?"

Kate ran to John's apartment and stepped through the open door. Peter was bent over the sofa, poking at the torn upholstery with the end of a pen. "Peter?" she called.

He stood and turned sharply. "Kate, you shouldn't be in here."

"It's the neighbor," Kate said. "Her door has been forced too."

Peter sprinted to the neighbor's door with Kate right behind him. He rushed through the open door. The woman lay sprawled on the floor of the living area. Peter dropped to his knees beside her and pressed his fingers to her neck. Kate held her breath and prayed.

"She has a pulse." He pointed at one of the uniformed officers. "Call an ambulance." He looked at Jim. "Do you know her name?"

Jim shook his head. "Didn't you interview her when you were here last?"

Peter shook his head. "Not yet; she wasn't home. It was on my follow-up list."

Kate walked to the dining room table where she saw a

scattering of mail and a checkbook. The woman had clearly been in the process of balancing her checkbook. She leaned over without touching anything and looked. "Her name is Esther Winn."

Peter nodded his thanks then leaned back over the unconscious woman. "Miss Winn? Miss Winn?" He got no answer. "I don't see any sign of injury."

The woman opened her eyes a crack and sucked in a harsh breath. It was clear she was in pain.

"Miss Winn?" Peter said. "What's wrong?"

She clutched at the front of her blouse. "Meds. Purse."

A purse lay on the table next to the checkbook, so Kate rooted quickly through it until she found a prescription medication bottle. She carried it to Peter. He read the label, shook out a pill, and slipped it into Miss Winn's mouth. The woman's pained panting evened out slightly.

"I think she's having a heart attack," Peter said. "Miss Winn, what happened?"

She closed her eyes and winced at the pain. She opened them long enough to gasp, "Bad men." Then she moaned and closed her eyes again. Her face was still twisted in pain, but she didn't reopen her eyes, even when Peter repeatedly called her name.

The EMTs arrived moments later. Kate wrung her hands while they loaded the woman onto a gurney. Miss Winn's face was pale as a ghost before they covered it with an oxygen mask and rushed her out.

"Do you think she'll live?" Kate asked Peter as he walked over to her side.

"I don't know, but I don't like the way this case is racking up damage and bodies. I want you to steer clear of this, Kate. Stay away before it's you I have to send to the hospital. I mean it!"

Ten

Peter turned to look at Jim and Alice fiercely. "All of you need to stay out of this before you get hurt. Leave the investigation to the police, *please.*"

Kate didn't like seeing Peter appeal to her friends to keep her out of trouble. She wasn't a kid who needed the grown-ups to look after her. It wasn't like their return to the apartment house had had anything to do with the destruction of John's apartment or the neighbor's attack. "As it turns out, it's a good thing we were here. Miss Winn might have died."

"Which I'm sure she'll appreciate," Peter said, clearly making a gigantic effort to keep his tone calm, "but I don't value her over you."

Jim thumped his cane lightly against the floor and all eyes turned to him. "Look, I hate to interrupt the beginnings of a lovers' quarrel, but I think we should come clean about a few things. We might know what the men who broke into the apartment were looking for."

Peter turned to look at him with interest. "Our search for John, *before we knew he was dead*, did turn up something," Jim said. "A folder. It's out in Alice's car. John kept it hidden between the mattress and box springs on his bed."

"How would you know what was hidden in his bed?" Peter asked.

"It turned up," Jim said with a shrug, "during our search for John."

"Well, I need to see it now," Peter said tightly.

As they walked out to the car, Kate noticed that the breeze had picked up and the sky looked like rain. She knew better than to expect it, though, with the dry weather they'd been having. Still, the darker sky made the wind sharper, and she wrapped her arms around herself for warmth as they walked. Peter took a step closer to her as if he might put a warming arm around her, but instead he simply walked at her side, blocking some of the chill breeze blowing across the parking lot.

Jim quickly retrieved the folder from the front seat of the car and handed it over. "They're not the most compelling photos I've ever seen."

Kate waited for him to hand over the flash drive as well, but noticed he didn't bring it up. She frowned at Jim, and he gave her an innocent smile.

Peter flipped through the folder. "Were there any papers with this? Something to explain the significance of the photos?"

Jim shook his head. "You're seeing the folder exactly the way we found it. Do you know any of these men?"

Peter peered at the faces and then shook his head. "If any of them are criminals, they aren't any I've come across. These look like photos from a jobsite. The logo is vaguely familiar though. I've seen it on trucks somewhere. I'm sure I can find someone at the station who'll recognize it." He looked up from the photos. "You're a professional photographer. Anything jump out at you when you looked at them?"

Jim shook his head. "Not much. They were clearly taken with a telephoto lens. The photographer probably wasn't visible to the subjects even though those are close up on some of the faces. But there's too much blurring whenever anyone moved. Whoever took the pictures wasn't a professional."

Peter looked at Alice. "You think it could have been your ex who took the photos?"

"Maybe. I don't know. We didn't see a camera in his apartment. Maybe he took them with his phone."

Jim shook his head at that. "No, they were taken with a decent digital camera."

"So, someone may have taken the camera when they took John," Peter said. "We still have no idea what that was about, though these photos may be a good bet."

"You knew John was seeing Elina Vasin?" Alice asked.

"Yes," Peter said, his voice turning sharp again. He let his gaze sweep over all of them. "You all need to stay away from her. You definitely do not want to be on that woman's radar. The Vasins are dangerous people."

Kate felt her face warm when he turned to her. "Uh ..."

Peter groaned. "You've been to see her?"

Alice spoke, drawing his attention away from Kate. "We have, but we parted under pleasant terms, so I think we're all right. She's interesting. At any rate, she said John was in the middle of some scheme that he believed would make him wealthy. I wonder if these photos are related to that scheme. Knowing John as I did, I would imagine that blackmail was involved."

Peter looked back down at the photos in his hand. "Usually blackmail photos are a lot seedier."

"There must be some reason why John hid them under his mattress."

Peter nodded. "I'll see what I can find out. In the meantime, I strongly recommend you stay away from the Vasin family. People who annoy them usually end up hurt or missing."

"We're doing our best not to be annoying," Jim said.

Peter gave them another lecture about interfering in the investigation and then looked pointedly at Jim and waved the folder. "Is there anything else you want to tell me?"

"Not at the moment."

Before Peter could reply, Kate put her hand on his arm. "Could you let me know about Miss Winn when you find out?"

"Kate ..."

"Not about the case," Kate added. "I met her, and I just want to know if she's all right. I liked her."

Peter nodded. "I'll let you know. I have to get back to my team. Please, stay out of trouble."

"We always *try* to stay out of trouble," Alice insisted.

Peter just groaned again and walked back to the apartment building. Once he was inside, Alice turned to look at Jim. "And how happy do you suppose he'd be if he knew we were still withholding evidence?"

"You're referring to the phone and flash drive, I assume?" Jim asked. "I'm just keeping things in the hands of the people most likely to get answers from them. The flash drive and phone are useless without passwords. And who would be more likely to figure out the passwords than the man's ex-wife?"

"I don't know ... maybe an expert in the technology?" Alice asked.

"Fine, we'll compromise. If we can't figure out the password in the next twenty-four hours, we'll hand it all over to Peter." He thought about that for a moment and added, "Anonymously." He rubbed his hands together. "I assume Kate knows where he lives, and I could pick the lock on his truck and just leave the stuff on his seat."

"I'm sure he'd never think of *us* in that situation," Alice said dryly as she hauled open the car door.

"What he thinks and what he can prove are two totally different things."

"So, where to next?" Alice asked when they'd piled into the car.

Jim twisted around slightly in his seat. "Kate, your friend

in the hotel business—can we take the photos over to show them to her?"

"You handed them over to Peter."

"They also exist on your computer. We can pick it up and take it to your friend's hotel. We need a lead to discover who those men are."

"I hate to bother her at work again," Kate said. "I could call and have her meet us at my house after she gets off work."

"That should be fine. So, where do we spend the next few hours until Kate's friend gets off work?" Jim asked.

Alice pulled out into traffic. "Let's find out how long that'll be first. Kate, can you call Vivi?"

Kate dug her phone out of her purse and used her speed-dial to call her friend. As she placed the call, she heard Alice say, "Jim? Do you see those cargo vans behind us? Do they look suspicious to you?"

"They're ugly, but beyond that, I assume there are hundreds of those things in a big city like Fort Worth."

"Maybe," Alice said. "But they pulled out of parking spots right next to the apartments at the same time we pulled out, and they've been behind us ever since."

Jim shrugged. "Maybe they're going our way."

"Maybe."

Kate twisted in her seat to look behind her at the same time that Vivi picked up her phone. "Kate!" her friend said. "Don't tell me you need rescuing again."

"No, I'm fine," Kate said. "I have some photos I want to show you. Can you come by my house after work?"

"Sure," Vivi said. "Actually, my afternoon meeting with the head of that business group I told you about had to cancel, so I'll be leaving here in an hour or so."

When Kate finished the call, she passed the information on.

"Since it won't be long," Jim said, "we could go back to your house."

"Good idea," Alice said as she gave another worried glance in her side mirrors. "Maybe we can stay out of trouble that way."

They drove without speaking for about ten minutes. Alice glanced frequently into the rearview mirror, and Kate noticed that Jim was beginning to watch the traffic in the side mirror. Kate shifted in her seat so that she could look out the rear window. She saw that traffic had thinned a bit, which made the two vans stand out all the more.

"Those vans are definitely following us," Alice said.

Jim shifted in his seat to look out the back window. "I noticed. We should lead them somewhere besides Kate's house."

"That's what I'm thinking." Alice turned the wheel sharply to the right, swinging the convertible into a tight turn. Kate looked out the back window again. The closest van couldn't make the turn fast enough and missed them, but the other was still following. Alice made a turn at every intersection, sometimes illegally. Traffic thinned more and more as her choices took them into less appealing areas of the city.

"I don't want to cramp your style, Red, but I think we should head for busier streets."

"I don't know this town," Alice said as she swung into a wide left turn, making the single battered Chevy in the oncoming lane honk and swerve. "I'm making random choices here. Maybe you could use your phone to plot a course?"

Jim pulled his phone from his jacket pocket as Alice turned right at the next intersection. The van hung on their tail like a burr on a dog's coat.

"All right," Jim said. "I think I can see the way to go, just don't take the next—"

Alice wrenched the wheel sharply, and the convertible lunged into a tight right turn.

"—right."

"Oops," Alice said as the street ahead of them ended in a rubble-strewn empty lot. She swung the convertible into a U-turn, but the street behind them was already blocked by the van. "That can't be good."

The second van, which they thought they'd lost long before, turned onto the street. "It's not getting any better either," Jim said.

The side doors on the vans swung open and five men jumped out, all wearing ski masks and carrying guns.

"And it keeps getting worse!" Alice yelled. She slammed the car into reverse and hit the gas. The convertible jumped away from the men with guns as Alice raced backward into the empty lot. The men shouted at them and waved the guns in the air but never fired.

The Mustang bumped and scraped across the lot, and Kate felt a stir of hope in the middle of her panic until one of the rear wheels hit a hole. The car came to a dead stop. Alice rocked the car back and forth, trying to pull free, but she wasn't fast enough. The men reached the car and pointed guns at the windows.

"Get out!" one of them bellowed.

Eleven

The gunmen stood well clear of the doors, but they kept their guns trained on Kate and her friends. Kate looked from man to man, searching for any clues as to who they might be. She couldn't tell much. Enough skin showed around the holes of the ski masks to tell that the men were white. They moved like young men and seemed muscular, but their winter jackets made it hard to tell.

"Get out!" the leader shouted again. "Now!"

"Looks like we better do what they say, Red," Jim said.

Kate fought the urge to cry or scream and got out of the car with her friends. Four of the five armed men herded them away from the car. Then two of those stood glaring with their guns pointed at the group while the others searched the car. Apparently they didn't find what they wanted because one of the searchers stalked over to the group.

"Where is it?" he asked.

"I don't know what you're talking about," Jim answered. "What kind of 'it' do you want?"

The man merely growled and grabbed for Alice's purse. Alice held on a moment too long, and the man shoved the gun in her face. "Hey!" Jim yelled, wedging himself between the man and Alice. The man smacked Jim in the side of the head with his gun, knocking him down.

"Stop that!" Alice shouted, shoving her purse hard at the armed man. "Here's my purse." Then she dropped to her knees next to Jim.

Another man took Kate's bag, and they searched them both. Clearly not finding what they wanted, the men threw the purses on the ground in frustration.

"Forget John MacFarlane ever existed," one gunman said as he waved his gun back toward the vans, signaling the others to back off. "If not, you'll never make it to Christmas."

The men trotted back to the vans and screeched back down the dead-end street.

Alice looked up from Jim. "Call the police and an ambulance."

Kate scrambled for her purse to get her cellphone, but Jim waved one hand at her. He held his other hand against the side of his head; Kate could see blood trickling through his fingers. "I'm fine," he said. "Don't call anyone."

Alice leaned close and stared into his eyes. "Are you sure?"

"I'm fine," he said.

"Positive?" she asked.

"Yes, Red, I'm fine."

"Good," Alice said, and then she smacked him in the upper arm.

Jim yelped. "What did you do that for?"

"That's for getting in the way of a man with a gun. I'm not some delicate desert flower who needs you to rush in and rescue me." She smacked his arm again. "He could have shot you or bashed your head in."

"Or he could have bruised my arm!"

Since he insisted he was fine, Alice and Kate hauled Jim to his feet. Kate pulled a crisp, clean handkerchief trimmed with crochet lace from her purse and handed it to Jim. He looked at the scrap of fabric in surprise. "I always carry a handkerchief," she said. "Sometimes a tissue just isn't enough."

"I appreciate that," Jim said as he pressed the handkerchief against his head, wincing. He still seemed a little wobbly, so they each ducked under an arm to help him to the car. "Whoa, this whole injured hero stuff is looking up."

"You're not the hero," Alice said. "You're the guy who gets in the way and ends up knocked on the head."

"I was a little heroic," Jim grumbled.

"Sure," Alice said. While Jim stood leaning against the side of the car, she and Kate shoved some branches and debris under the wheel that had slipped into the deep pothole.

"I have a first-aid kit at home," Kate said when they finished and she climbed into the backseat. "But I still think we should have called Peter about this. One of us could have been badly hurt or worse."

"What are the police going to do?" Jim said as he eased into the front seat and fumbled with his seat belt with one hand still pressed to his head. "I didn't see anything that would clue us in on who those guys were. Plus, I'd like your boyfriend to forget all about me as quickly as possible."

"But wouldn't this clear you?" Kate asked. "Obviously, whoever killed John attacked us."

"Not necessarily," Alice said. She cranked the car and eased it out of the hole. "John probably upset a lot of people. The attack might not have been related to his death."

"Or it *might* have been," Kate said.

"Can we argue about it after I get some aspirin?" Jim asked.

They made the rest of the trip quietly, though Alice kept glancing Jim's way as she drove. Clearly she wasn't convinced that he was all right. When they finally reached Kate's house, Jim complained of a headache but was clearly far less wobbly when he walked.

Kate brought out her first-aid kit, and Jim eyed the large box. "You expecting some kind of medical emergency?"

"Harry's parents bought it for me when I decided to move to Texas," Kate said. "I guess they worried about accidents."

"It's nice that they still care," Alice said as Kate handed over a bottle of hydrogen peroxide from the kit. "Divorce can lead to a lot of blame placing." Alice soaked a gauze pad in the liquid and dabbed at Jim's wound while he winced.

Kate rooted through the kit for a bandage. "Harry's folks love him, but they don't have a lot of illusions about him."

"Must be nice. John was always the golden boy to his mother," Alice said, shaking her head. "No matter how many times he got into trouble, it was always someone else's fault. You wouldn't believe some of the crazy justifications she came up with. She died before we split up, but I know it would have been all my fault in her eyes."

Kate had never thought of her own divorce as being easy, but she realized that it certainly could have been much more difficult. She could still talk to Harry without fighting—most of the time. And his parents showed her the same respect and warmth as always. Realistically, things could have been much worse.

"Can you just put a bandage on that and stop fussing?" Jim asked after Alice had spent some more time dabbing at the cut. "I think it hurt less when the guy hit me."

"Fine. I think it's clean enough anyway." Alice taped on the bandage. "I'm going to take this old pirate back to the hotel so he can rest for a while. Can you call and let us know if Vivi recognizes anything from the photos?"

Kate was surprised when Jim didn't argue that he was well enough to stay. His head must have been hurting more than he liked to show. "I'll call as soon as I know anything," she promised.

Vivi showed up not long after Jim and Alice left. She was

carrying an armload of paperwork. As soon as Kate opened the front door, Vivi immediately began apologizing. "I got tied up with a sudden crisis. I'm so sorry. Are your friends here?"

"No, they went back to the hotel. Something happened after I talked to you on the phone." Kate went on to describe the harrowing experience as the two walked to the sofa and sat. As she talked, Vivi's blue eyes got wider and wider. For the first time, the real horror of what they'd been through hit Kate, and her hands began to shake.

"That sounds terrifying," Vivi said, wrapping an arm around her friend. "Are you all right?"

Kate nodded with a shaky smile. "Honestly, I think telling it scared me as much as being there. It happened so fast and then we were so worried about Jim, I barely had time to get scared."

"Are you sure Jim's all right?"

"I think he's in pain, but he should be fine. Clearly we've stepped into a hornet's nest with this whole business over Alice's ex. Plus, I discovered the phone call wasn't a prank; Elina was threatening me."

"Do you think Elina sent those men?" Vivi asked. "Or Serge?"

"I don't know. I do wonder if it might be related to something we found in John's apartment. The men today were definitely searching Alice's car for *something*. Would you look at something for me?" Kate stood and was relieved when her knees didn't shake.

"Of course." Vivi followed Kate to the kitchen where the laptop was still on the table. Kate booted up the computer and showed Vivi the photos. "These were in a file folder hidden under John's mattress. They don't look particularly sinister, but maybe they're what the men were after."

Vivi studied the photo on the screen. "This looks like a jobsite. It doesn't look particularly secret."

"But it was hidden under a mattress. Do you recognize anything or anyone?"

Vivi leaned close and pointed. "I know that truck. Well, the logo anyway. I've seen it on some of the materials I've gotten from that environmental business group."

"The one having a Christmas party at your hotel?" Kate asked.

Vivi nodded. "That the logo for Battmin's Manufacturing. Hold on, I'll show you." She set her folders and clipboard on the table and rooted through the material. Finally she pulled out a sheet of letterhead. "See?"

With the full logo showing, Kate was easily able to recognize it as the one on the truck. What had looked almost like stray lines were actually parts of a stylized leaf. "Have you met any of the people from the company?" Kate asked. "Do any of these men look familiar?"

Vivi frowned. "I'm not sure." She pointed at one man whose face was turned mostly away from the camera. "That could be Philip Battmin, but it could be almost any man of about that age too. I met Mr. Battmin a couple of times, and he has salt-and-pepper hair like that and wears it short, but ..." She shrugged.

"Knowing the logo is one more thing than we knew before," Kate said. "I wonder why John was hiding the photos."

"You don't think Mr. Battmin is involved in the murder, do you?" Vivi said. "He seems like a nice enough guy, and he's hugely into the environmental movement. He's very charming, though not really my type."

"I don't know. It's another piece of a very confusing puzzle. I just wish I could meet him."

Vivi's face brightened. "I can help with that."

"You can?"

She nodded. "Their holiday party is tomorrow. He's supposed to come early for a meeting in one of our conference rooms. I don't know why he doesn't just do that at his company offices, but if he wants to pay us, I'm not going to try to talk him out of it."

"So, you're going to smuggle me into the meeting?" Kate asked.

"Something like that," Vivi said with an impish grin. Then her face sobered. "Are you sure you want to be smuggled in? It might be safer just to step out of this."

"I think I'll feel safer when the killer is caught and not before," Kate said. "Part of me is sorry we ever started looking for John. But now we're in the middle of it, and I think we just have to sink or swim."

"In that case, I'm with you. Anything I can do to help is fine with me. You just show up at the hotel tomorrow and leave it to me." She gave Kate the particulars and then gathered up her papers. "I should get home. I still need to make a couple of calls and heat up some supper. Then I'm going to finish Mom's sweater!"

"That's the spirit," Kate said. "I need to put some more time into Vanessa's sweater as well. This has certainly been an unexpectedly busy holiday season so far."

Vivi rolled her eyes. "Tell me about it."

After her friend left, Kate considered calling Peter. Despite Jim's reluctance, she didn't feel completely comfortable about withholding what she knew about the case.

She gathered up her yarn and hook and settled down on the sofa to consider what she should do. She let the careful counting and the slip of the hook as it pulled the yarn through each stitch soothe her. The tension in her shoulders that she'd barely noticed seemed to ease. The experience with the gunmen had shaken her badly, and she needed to talk to Peter. It felt like the right thing to do. Jim had stated his preference that they avoid police attention, but Kate hadn't promised.

Once she chose her course of action, even more of her nervousness seemed to slip away, and she laid the sweater aside to make the call. Peter answered immediately. "Kate, I was just going to call you. I spoke to the doctor, and Miss Winn is going to be all right."

"I'm so glad." Kate felt a twinge of guilt. She'd forgotten all about the poor woman.

"I tried to talk to her, but she claims she doesn't remember a thing. She's scared. I could see it in her eyes. I didn't want to badger her, but I'm going to try again after she's had some time to rest."

"She went through a terrible ordeal," Kate said.

"I know. I'll try to be sensitive." Peter paused. "You don't sound mad at me anymore. I'm glad of that."

Now Kate spoke hesitantly. "Actually, I have something I need to tell you."

There was a pause before Peter spoke again. "I'm not going to like this, am I?"

"No."

"Should I come over?"

"No, just let me tell you." She took a deep breath and rushed through the narrative of events from the time they noticed the vans following them through the blow to Jim's head.

At that point, Peter interrupted for the first time, his voice tight. "Is he all right? Are *you* all right? I'm coming over."

"No, no. I'm fine, honestly," she said. "No one even touched me. They just searched my purse."

"And pointed guns at you! How about Jim?"

"I think he's fine. He didn't have any symptoms of a concussion except a little headache, and Alice bandaged the cut."

"This is exactly why you all can't be out there playing amateur detectives. This is a murder case. That means the people involved play rough."

"But Alice and Jim are part of the people involved," Kate said. "You dragged them downtown for questioning. How can you expect them not to feel involved?"

"What I'd like to know is why you didn't call me from the scene."

"Because my friends didn't want to spend the rest of the day answering questions when Jim had a headache, maybe. Because you treated them like murder suspects, so they don't exactly see you as someone to turn to for help. And because we didn't have anything useful to tell you. The men wore ordinary, nondescript clothes—jeans, plain jackets, dark ski masks. The cargo vans didn't have any markings. All calling you offered was more time at the police station."

"It offered you all the chance to be normal people," Peter said, his voice rising slightly. "Normal people call the police when someone threatens them with a gun. You could get hurt. You have to tell me about these things."

"I thought I was doing that. Maybe I was wrong."

Peter huffed in exasperation. "Right. I'm glad you called. I'm going to call to make sure you're still getting a patrol drive-by there. And *please* try to stay out of trouble."

"I'm not looking for trouble," Kate said.

"That's the problem. It seems to be looking for you."

Kate started to protest, but Peter shifted gears. He promised to get together to finish decorating the tree as soon as he caught a break in the case. "Have you heard from Vanessa?" he asked.

"Not today. I'm sure she's busy having fun with the family." Kate felt a pang. Vanessa was her family.

"She'll call soon."

"Probably." Kate wiped a finger across her suddenly wet eyelashes. "It's been a long day, and I need to go fix something to eat."

"Sure, of course. Take care." Peter hung on the phone another moment. "I wish I could come over."

"That's OK. I'm a little worn out for company anyway." Kate forced cheer into her voice. "Don't work too hard, and you stay safe too. I'll talk to you soon." Then she ended the call before Peter could come up with any new warnings. As she set the phone down on the table beside her, she realized she'd forgotten to tell him about the Battmin Manufacturing logo on the side of the trucks in the photo. She shrugged. If Vivi could figure it out, she was sure someone at the police station had as well. If she learned anything interesting at the hotel, she'd call him again.

With that resolved, she stretched and marched off to the kitchen to heat up a can of soup and pretend it was a healthy supper.

Twelve

By midmorning on Friday, Kate was standing nervously in a hallway at the Hamilton Arms Hotel. She tugged at the hem of the pinstriped vest she wore over a long-sleeved white blouse, part of the hotel's uniform for the staff.

Vivi swatted at her arm. "Stop fussing. You look fine."

Kate stared at the door to the small conference room. "What if some of the men who attacked Alice, Jim, and me are in there? They'll recognize me."

"Not in that wig and those glasses," Vivi assured her. "I barely recognize you. Besides, these movers and shakers never pay attention to the waitstaff."

Kate put a hand up to touch the headful of springy curls. Vivi had brought the wig and glasses from home to complete the disguise. They'd been part of Halloween costumes from past years. "Is the wig straight?"

"Yes, it's fine," Vivi whispered as she gave Kate a light push toward the door. "Just slip in, put this water pitcher on the table at the back of the room, fiddle around with the snacks a little, and leave when you've gotten a good look at everyone."

"Right," Kate said, her voice barely audible. She put a little more energy into it. "Right." She turned panicky eyes toward Vivi. "Are you going to wait out here?"

"I shouldn't. It'll look weird. I'll go back to my office. Join me when you're done and tell me all about it." Vivi handed her the pitcher of water.

Kate nodded. Then she forced herself to reach out and

turn the door handle to the conference room. When she stepped in, most of the men at the table glanced in her direction, but when they saw the uniform, they all returned their focus to the meeting.

The pitcher shook slightly in her hand as Kate walked quickly to the table. She managed to slosh only a little as she set the pitcher on the table. Then she quickly covered the damp spot with a few napkins. She moved plates of muffins and other pastries around a little as she cast glances toward the table, looking for faces from the file of photos.

She recognized Battmin from the website. He could have been the man Vivi had pointed out in one of the photos, but Kate had no way to be sure. He had the same close-cropped graying hair and tan.

She turned her attention to the other men at the table and quickly recognized one of them from the photo, a lanky man who looked ill at ease in the suit he wore. In the photo he'd worn jeans and a work shirt, but she was sure it was the same man. He shifted uncomfortably in his seat. His restless movements and slightly bored frown gave the impression of a man who definitely didn't want to be there.

Picking up a plate of tiny quiches, Kate looked for a spot on the table to shift it to. At exactly that moment, the fidgeting man spoke loudly, asking Battmin whether he'd made a decision about some work-site crisis. Startled, Kate nearly dumped the tiny quiches onto the table. She recognized that voice. In fact, she'd never forget it. It was the voice of the man who'd struck Jim!

When Battmin answered, his voice didn't seem familiar at all. Of course, some of the men who'd attacked them hadn't spoken, so that didn't rule out Battmin from being among them. Even if he hadn't been there, he still could have sent the gunmen to keep his own hands clean. Kate forced herself to keep fiddling with the refreshments for a few minutes more, listening to the different men speak. The loud man spoke again, and Kate had no doubt. She had to find out who the man was so she could tell Peter.

She slipped out of the room and practically ran to Vivi's office. When she flung open the door, she found the office empty. Kate perched on the end of Vivi's desk and called her cell.

"Kate?" Vivi said.

"I'm in your office. I recognized the voice of one of the men in the meeting. I need you to tell me who it is."

"Fine. I'll meet you back in the hall. Their scheduled time is almost up. You can point the man out as they leave, and I'll let you know if I recognize him. Did you snap a photo with your cell, just in case?"

"No," Kate moaned. "I didn't think of it."

"We'll do that too. I'm heading to the hall now."

Kate hurried back through the halls even faster on the return trip and collected a few admonishing looks. She reached the hall outside the meeting room just moments before the door opened and the men inside began to file out. Not wanting to draw their attention, Kate slowed as she walked to Vivi.

Vivi turned questioning eyes toward Kate and pulled out her cellphone, holding it up as if showing something to Kate. As each man left the room, Vivi snapped a photo. The loud man and Battmin were the last two out of the meeting room. Battmin spotted Vivi and smiled brightly at her. Vivi returned the smile as she dropped the phone back into the pocket of her blazer.

Battmin walked over with the loud man following behind. "This room was perfect for our needs," he said. "Do you have everything you need for the party on Monday?"

Vivi's smile turned up to full wattage. "Yes, I do, Mr. Battmin. I believe you'll be very happy."

"I'm sure I will," he said agreeably. Then he turned to the man beside him. "Walk out with me, Edgar. We need to discuss a few things."

The other man nodded. His eyes swept briefly over Kate, and she nearly shuddered from the fear that he would recognize her, but he seemed uninterested. He followed Battmin down the hall.

"Do you know who he is?" Kate whispered as she followed Vivi into the empty meeting room. "The Edgar guy?"

Vivi stacked the empty ceramic mugs from the conference table. "Edgar Henderson. He owns Eagle Shipping."

"Eagle Shipping?" Kate's eyes widened in recognition. "Would that be 'eagle' as in Eagle Mountain Lake where John's body was found?"

"The same," Vivi said. She dropped her voice to a bare whisper. "Do you think he could be the killer?"

"I don't know." Kate piled more mugs onto Vivi's tray. "I should go and call Peter as soon as we finish cleaning up."

Vivi shook her head. "Don't worry about that. Someone will be along to help any second. I'm not usually the one who does this anyway. Go and make the call. You can use my office if you want some privacy."

"Thanks," Kate said. "You're a gem." She left the room and headed for Vivi's office, this time walking at a respectable pace. She reached the lobby and was on her way across when she spotted a familiar face coming in the front door. "Peter! What are you doing here? Did you figure out about Battmin Manufacturing too?"

"If you mean did I identify the logo on the truck, yes," he said. "But I'm here for something unrelated. What does this hotel have to do with Battmin Manufacturing?" He looked at her from curly head to toe. "And why are you dressed like that? Are you moonlighting?"

"The hotel is hosting their holiday party," Kate said. "And some of the men involved had a meeting here this morning. Vivi loaned me the uniform and the wig so I could slip in and see if I recognized anyone from the photos."

"The photos you don't have anymore," Peter said.

"Good memory." Kate stepped close. "I recognized one of the men," she whispered, "but not from the photo. He was one of the gunmen who attacked us yesterday. He was the one who hit Jim."

Peter's expression darkened. "I thought you said the men wore masks."

"They did, but I recognized his voice."

"His voice?" Peter frowned. "I'm not sure I can bring someone in based on that. Did he really say enough for a positive identification?"

"I'm sure it's the same man."

"Do you have any idea who he is?"

"Edgar Henderson. Vivi said he owns Eagle Shipping."

"I'll look into it." Peter sighed. "Finding you in costume here clearly means you're not going to do as I asked and stay out of trouble. How do you suppose the guy felt about seeing you here? You're painting a target on yourself, and I don't like it."

Kate shook her head. "He didn't seem to recognize me. That's what the wig was for."

That brought a slight smile to Peter's face, and he reached out to wrap one of the bouncy curls around one finger. "The wig is certainly a big change, but it's still *you* under there."

"He wasn't focused on me yesterday," Kate said. "Jim drew

most of the attention to himself after the guy threatened Alice."

"I'll look into it as soon as I'm done here. You should stay away from this hotel if that guy is going to be back here for a party. I'll take your word for it that he didn't recognize you, but you don't want to keep putting yourself in front of him."

"I'm leaving right now," Kate assured him. Of course she didn't tell him that she intended to go straight to Jim and Alice's hotel and tell them what she'd learned.

Peter reached out and caught her hand as she edged past him toward the exit. "I'll come over tonight, no matter what."

"That would be nice," she said.

He gestured at her outfit. "It would be a good idea to stay in the disguise until you get out of here."

Kate looked down at herself and felt warmth flood her cheeks. "Right. I'll change back at Alice's hotel. Then I'll give it all back to Vivi later."

"Good idea." He squeezed her hand and let it go.

Kate called Alice to tell her she'd discovered something and was going to come over.

"Terrific," Alice said. "Then we can go have lunch together."

The drive to the hotel was short, and Kate was soon pouring out what she'd learned to her friends. Jim rubbed lightly at the bandage on his forehead. "I'm not sure I like you taking that kind of risk," he said.

"I wore a disguise," Kate assured him. "There was no sign that the man recognized me, but we now know that the person who attacked us yesterday is somehow connected to that file of photos."

"Is he in the photos?" Alice asked.

Kate nodded. "Yes. He was dressed differently, but I clearly recognized his voice, and Vivi identified him as Edgar Henderson. I think Battmin might be in one of the photos too, but it's hard to tell. One of the men who never looks toward the camera has the same kind of hair. But we do know that the logo on those trucks is Battmin Manufacturing. And someone Battmin knows attacked us."

Jim got up from the sofa and walked over to the tiny desk to retrieve the copies of the photos that they'd printed out at Kate's house. He shook his head as he walked. "I don't know, Kate. The connections are pretty weak. I expect your boyfriend would agree with me."

"He does," Kate said.

Jim looked at her sharply. "You've talked to him?"

"I had to. This is a murder investigation. I couldn't withhold that kind of information, and he really doesn't suspect you and Alice."

Jim harrumphed. "You could have fooled me."

Alice took the photos from him and handed them to Kate. "Show us Edgar Henderson and the man that you think might be Battmin." Kate did, and then she studied each photo, comparing them mentally with the men she'd seen at the meeting. None of the other people looked familiar to her, though she felt more and more that the man with his face turned away really was Battmin.

Finally Jim said, "I think we should drive to both Battmin Manufacturing and this Eagle Shipping and look around a little. They're the only leads we have at the moment."

"Fine," Alice said. "But I want to grab something to eat on the way out of town. One of us didn't eat everything on the breakfast buffet this morning."

Jim chuckled. "One thing I've learned from all the traveling on photo expeditions: When food is available, eat it. You never know when you'll have time to stop again."

"We'll make time," Alice insisted. And they did, grabbing submarine sandwiches and cold drinks before driving north toward Eagle Mountain Lake and the shipping company. Since they knew the owner of Eagle Shipping had been involved in the attack on them and the lake was where John's body was recovered, it seemed the most likely location to find more clues.

When they reached the shipping company, they found that the whole business was surrounded by a tall chain-link fence and a wide double gate let vehicles in and out only after a guard checked a list. "I'm willing to bet we're not on the list," Jim said when Alice pulled off the road a short distance from the gate.

"I imagine you're right," Alice agreed. "So, I say we find a less open place to leave the car and we go for a little hike. We might not be able to get in, but we can see through the fence. We might see someone else from the photos."

"Sounds like a plan," Jim agreed. He looked over his shoulder into the back of the car. "You up for it, Kate? You've already had an adventurous morning."

She tried to sound more confident than she felt. "I'm good to go."

Jim used his phone to check satellite maps of the area and found an unmarked dirt road that they hadn't noticed on the drive up. It circled partly around the land on which the shipping company was situated. "This looks like a great place to hide the car."

They found the road easily enough, though driving it was a different matter. It clearly wasn't used much and was both overgrown and pitted. Alice gripped the steering wheel with white knuckles as she wrestled the car over the bumps and holes.

They finally pulled off where the car would be half covered by the overhanging branches of two massive pines. "The walk isn't far," Jim said as he eyed the area dubiously. "But I'm not sure how well I'll do."

"You could stay with the car," Alice suggested.

Jim shook his head. "I'll give it a try at least. If it gets rough, I can come back and wait."

They discovered a deer trail not far from the car that offered fairly smooth walking most of the way. When they reached the fence, Jim pulled out his phone so they could match any faces they might see with the photos from the apartment.

Kate looked at the phone in surprise. "When did you put the photos on your phone?"

"Before we handed them over to your boyfriend. I wanted to be sure to have them with me whenever we might need them."

Though they did see a few men, they were too far away for any positive identification.

"I don't think this is going to do us any good," Alice said, but Jim grabbed her arm and pointed.

"Look at that truck over there next to the block building. See anything unusual about it?" he asked.

Kate leaned closer to the fence to look. At first the truck seemed like any other, a heavy vehicle with thick wheels. Then she yelped. "The mud flaps don't match!"

"No, they don't," Jim said with a smirk. "One of them is that weird purple color. Look here." He held up the phone and they saw the back corner of a truck that showed an unusual purple mud flap. "We may not have seen any people from the photo, but this truck was definitely there."

"We have to get inside," Alice said. "That's not enough information."

Jim gave her a sideways glance. "What do you recommend?"

"What if Kate and I head to the gate on foot?" Alice suggested. "We could say that our car broke down and we need to use their phone because we can't get service. That would put us inside the gate, anyway."

"But I doubt it would put you very far inside, and I don't like you going without me."

"I'm counting on their big, manly chivalry kicking in when they see two stranded women," Alice said. "And that's not going to happen if you come along."

"What if their big, manly kidnapping urges kick in?" Jim asked.

Alice shrugged as she headed for the gate. "You can watch from the bushes and call the police if we don't come back out."

"That's a terrible plan," Jim said, turning to Kate even as he trailed along behind Alice. "Tell her that's a terrible plan."

"It's a scary plan," Kate agreed. *And Peter would hate it.* "But we might learn something."

They were about halfway to the gate—and Jim and Alice were still arguing—when Kate spotted flashing lights coming down the main road. She grabbed Alice's arm and pointed. Police cars, some marked and some not, came around the last curve and drove up to the gate of the shipping company. Kate sucked in a startled breath and took a step back when the first car stopped and Peter got out.

They were too far away to hear what Peter said as he held up a document in front of the gate guard, but the man quickly let them inside. "He must have had a warrant," Jim whispered. "I'd like to get in there now."

Alice leaned back against the fence, making it shake slightly. "I'm sure he'll just invite us right in."

Kate took a deep breath. "I should go try, anyway."

She took a step toward the gate, but Jim caught her arm. "Don't bother. He'll stick you in one of the cars to keep you safe. Do you think he'll tell you what he found?"

"I don't know. Maybe." She doubted it.

"I think we need to make better use of our time," Jim said. "Let's stay with the plan and go check out Battmin Manufacturing."

Kate looked at the group of cars. "I need to tell him to check out the truck with the mud flap. He could miss it, and he's right there."

Jim rubbed his beard. "Fine, but don't put yourself in the position of getting shoved into a car with an officer to baby-sit you. Call him or text him."

Kate was surprised when Peter picked up the phone. "Kate, I'm in the middle of something," he said.

"I know. I just wanted to tell you to check the mud flaps on the trucks. One has a single purple mud flap that matches a truck in the photos exactly."

"How do you know that?" Peter asked suspiciously.

"I just know. Check it. That truck was in the photos."

"Kate, if you're here somewhere ..."

"Just check. I have to go." She ended the call, and they trooped back to Alice's car. Kate half-expected Peter to call her right back, but he didn't. She hoped he found evidence that would clear Alice and Jim once and for all.

The drive to Battmin Manufacturing meant backtracking toward Fort Worth, but it didn't take long. As with the shipping company, the factory was fenced. It had several gates and guardhouses. However, as they watched a car pull in, they saw that the guards didn't check a list.

"I think I see a way in," Alice said. Then she gave Jim a smile. "It involves a little subterfuge."

"Another use of feminine wiles?" he asked.

"Something like that." She looked over her shoulder. "We can pretend our husbands work inside and they forgot their dinners. We'll use the bags from the submarine shop as a bluff. It might buy our way in."

"But we don't know the names of anyone who works there," Kate said.

"Look at the size of that place," Alice nodded toward the factory. "How could the gate guards know everyone?"

Jim sighed and swung open his car door. "Sounds risky, but it might work. I'll wait here, but not long. You two get in and out quick or I'm calling Kate's boyfriend."

"No problem." Alice hopped out of the car. "This is going to be a piece of cake."

Kate got out more slowly, looking nervously toward the factory. She just hoped this piece of cake didn't turn deadly.

Thirteen

The guard who walked toward Alice's car looked barely older than Vanessa. He had a friendly smile and a bit of a swagger as he approached. "Can I help you, ladies?"

"I hope so." Alice held up a sandwich bag and Kate mimicked her. "We made our husbands help with Christmas shopping before work, and they managed to forget their dinners. Can we bring them in?"

The young man laughed. "I guess so. Making them go shopping *and* miss their supper would be too cruel."

"Hey, shopping is fun," Alice said, joining in the young man's laughter.

Kate tried to laugh too, but nerves made it come out a little squeaky.

"What department are your husbands in?" the young man asked.

Kate nearly squeaked again. *What department?* She had no idea what departments might be in there.

"Maintenance," Alice said.

The young man winced. "Poor guys. I heard they were cleaning stacks today. Go on around to the far doors. You should be able to leave their dinners in the break room. Just put their names on them."

"Thanks." Alice drove past the guardhouse, following the road that the young man had pointed out.

"How did you come up with a department so fast?" Kate asked. "I thought I was going to pass out when he asked that."

Alice shrugged. "Every company has a maintenance department." She pulled her phone out of her pocket. "I want to be ready if we need to take a photo."

As they walked in the heavy door, Kate tried to mimic Alice's confident stride. When they stepped into the break room, Kate had to stifle a gasp. A small group of men sat around a table, sipping coffee, and Kate recognized two of the men from the photos.

Kate looked quickly at Alice and saw her friend had held the phone up near her ear and was nodding as if someone was speaking to her. But the phone was tilted slightly toward the table.

One of the men from the tables stood, and Kate noticed he was trying to pull in his sizable stomach. "Are you two new? I'm sure I'd have remembered seeing two such lovely ladies."

"Careful, Ralph," one of the seated men said, smacking him on the arm. "You'll be back in sensitivity training."

Ralph gave his friend a glare. "It's not insensitive to recognize beauty."

Kate noticed that the two men she recognized from the photos didn't join in the conversation. She smiled nervously. "I think we might have the wrong break room."

"This is the only break room at this end of the floor," Ralph said. "Would you like a seat?" He pulled out his own chair and gestured toward it.

"No thanks," Alice said. "Actually, I just remembered something I forgot in the car. My hearing protectors."

"I never use those," Ralph said. "The machines aren't that loud."

"Better safe than sorry," Alice said as they backed toward the door.

One of the men who hadn't spoken yet stood, looking at them intently. "We didn't get your names."

Alice said, "That's because we weren't giving them out."

"What department do you work in?" the man asked as he circled the table.

"We work in the mind-your-own-business department," Alice said. Kate wasn't sure that provoking the man was the right choice in the situation. "We'll see you guys around."

Then Alice turned as if she didn't have a care in the world and hustled Kate out of the room. As soon as they got clear of the doorway, Alice picked up speed. Kate was happy to trot along with her. When they reached the heavy outside door, she glanced back to see the man from the photo standing in the doorway of the break room, watching them leave. He had a cellphone at his ear.

"I think one of the guys may be telling on us," Kate said as soon as they got outside.

"Then we should move right along." Alice broke into a sprint, and they raced for the car. She drove back to the gate as fast as she could manage wisely. As they passed the guardhouse, the young man stepped out and yelled at them to wait. Alice ignored him and they sailed away.

They picked up Jim and didn't stop again until they reached Sage Hills. Jim was interested to hear that two of the men from the photo were definitely part of Battmin Manufacturing.

"Do you think they recognized you?" Jim asked. "They could have been some of the thugs."

"I don't think so," Kate said. "It seems like he would have made more of an effort to keep us there or would have called for someone to stop us more quickly. He was suspicious, but he didn't act like he knew who we were."

"I agree with Kate," Alice said. "But I also think Battmin Manufacturing and Eagle Shipping are behind John's death, and it's all about those photos. I just don't know why."

Kate sat back in the seat. There was no doubt that they'd identified some of the companies involved in the photos. And someone wanted the photos back badly. But if they were willing to kill John to get them, why hadn't they been more aggressive when they'd accosted Kate, Alice, and Jim the day before?

When they pulled up at Kate's house, Alice turned in her seat. "Do you think you could call Peter and see what he knows?"

"Or at least what he's willing to tell you?" Jim said. "We need to know that before we plan our next move."

"He promised to come by tonight," Kate said. "But I don't know how much he'll tell me. I *will* ask."

"The answer to everything is wrapped up in those photos," Jim said. "I'm sure of it."

Kate was less sure, but she wasn't certain why. With nothing else to offer, she promised to call them as soon as she spoke to Peter. When she got out of the car and walked up to her door, she realized how glad she was to be home. She found adventures and mysteries much more appealing in theory. In practice, they seemed to bounce her from one terrifying moment to another.

Kate settled down in her cozy crocheting chair with a cup of tea and Vanessa's Christmas present. She'd only finished a few rows when the phone rang. With a sinking heart, Kate grabbed her purse. She expected the call to be Peter begging off on his promised visit. Instead, she saw Vanessa's name on the phone.

"Hi, sweetheart," Kate said happily. "How are you?"

"I'm missing you. Dad said he talked to you," Vanessa said. "I wish he'd waited until I was back so I could have talked to you then. Nana and Papa have been great. And Dad's trying.

It's good to see my Stony Point friends, but it's not the same. I threw a clump of tinsel at Nana's tree, and I thought she would pass out."

It warmed Kate to know Vanessa was also missing their traditions. "Sometimes we have to roll with it," she said. Then she laughed. "Sounds like Nana would like Peter. He thinks tossed tinsel clumps are evil too."

"They're the best part of tree decorating," Vanessa said. "You cannot let him talk you out of flinging tinsel."

"No chance," Kate said. "I'm a tinsel flinger forever."

They talked for a while about other favorite Christmas moments before Vanessa asked Kate to hold on for a moment. Kate heard Vanessa's voice slightly muffled as she yelled, "I'll be right there, Nana!"

When Vanessa came back to the phone, Kate said, "I know. You have to go."

"We're heading over to Maplehurst Inn," Vanessa said. "They're having a Christmas dinner theater thing. Some of the high school kids are doing a readers' theater performance of *A Christmas Carol*."

"Sounds like fun."

"Sure, they start doing fun things *after* I graduate," Vanessa said. Kate heard a voice in the background. "I really have to go now," her daughter said. "I'll call again soon. I love you, Mom."

"I love you too, sweetheart," Kate said. "Do me one favor though. Don't talk about Peter around your dad, OK?"

"I won't. It makes him sulky anyway. Gotta go. Bye."

When the call ended, Kate held the phone in her hand, feeling the bittersweet mix of joy at talking to Vanessa and the lingering pain of missing her.

The knock at the door came less than an hour later. Kate had returned to her crocheting enthusiastically, picturing the joy on Vanessa's face when she came home and they had their gift exchange. Kate folded the sweater carefully and slipped it into her project bag. Then she opened the door to greet Peter.

He looked tired. The normal lines from years of Texas sun seemed a little deeper, but when he saw Kate, his smile lifted some of the weariness away. "Hi."

"Hi yourself," Kate said. "Are you here to yell at me?"

"You mean about your skulking around Eagle Shipping?" Peter shook his head. "I don't have the energy to yell. Besides, after the day I've had, I don't need to lose my one fan."

"Do you want to come in and talk about it?"

He nodded, and she stepped aside. His walk held a bit less of his normal cowboy swagger, and he stopped by the Christmas tree. "We really do need to get together and finish this."

"I like it," Kate said. "Especially the tinsel bombs."

"We'll talk about the tinsel bombs." He gave her a pitiful look. "Could I have some coffee? And a sandwich? It's been one of those days."

"Of course, though I should make decaf so you're not up half the night."

He groaned as he followed Kate to the kitchen. "I may be anyway. This case is frustrating. As you know, we searched Eagle Shipping today. The techs found some trace blood evidence, though we don't have a clear DNA match to prove it's John's blood."

"But it's blood, which means he died at the shipping company?" Kate opened the cupboard to retrieve the decaf coffee.

"I don't think so. There was very little blood and no sign of cleanup. A chest wound would have bled a lot more than that. What I do suspect is that he may have gotten his beating there, though no one is admitting to anything at this point. When we showed the photos to Edgar Henderson, he said they just proved MacFarlane was trespassing on the grounds and that's probably how he got hurt."

"So the photos *were* taken at Eagle Shipping?" Kate said.

"According to Henderson, but I don't know. I have no evidence that he was lying. His statement is plausible, and our techs can't find anything shady about the photos. We haven't identified all the men yet. But still, it doesn't look like anything sinister was happening."

With the coffee brewing, Kate opened the fridge and piled sandwich makings on the counter. She glanced sideways at Peter. "I saw two more of the men today," she said casually.

Peter's eyes lit up. "Is that meat loaf? I love meat loaf." He hung over her shoulder as she cut off a thick slice for his sandwich. "You saw two more of the men when you were risking life and limb at the shipping company?"

She shook her head and considered waving the meat loaf under his nose to keep him distracted. "Actually, I saw them at Battmin Manufacturing."

Peter froze. "You were at Battmin Manufacturing?"

"Briefly," Kate said. "With Alice. We saw a couple of the men from the photos." She offered him the sandwich.

He hesitated before taking it. "I should arrest you all and keep you in holding until I get to the bottom of this, just for my own peace of mind." Kate started to pull the sandwich back, and Peter snatched it from her hands. "You're lucky I'm starving and not thinking straight."

"On the upside, we know both Battmin Manufacturing and Eagle Shipping are in the photos."

"True," Peter said. "But since the photos seem to be benign, I still don't know why they wanted them back so badly. There's no reason the two companies couldn't work together. They're part of the same group."

Kate poured coffee into two mugs, and they sat down at the cozy kitchen table. Peter took a deep sip. "Basically I'm stuck, unless Jim wants to press charges for the assault. If he does, I can haul Edgar Henderson in and put him in a lineup."

"Which won't be very helpful since we didn't see any of their faces."

"True, but if Jim recognizes Henderson's voice, I can hold him. I probably can't get a conviction based on it, but I can hold him. And possibly sweat some straight answers out of him."

Kate pondered that while she sipped her coffee. "I don't know if Jim would be open to that," she said finally, "but I can ask him."

"Tell him it's my only play at the moment."

"I will."

Kate set her mug back on the table, and Peter reached out to cover her hand with his. "How are you doing?" he asked. "I haven't had a minute to ask. Investigation aside, is having Jim and Alice around helping?"

"In some ways," Kate said. "I'm starting to see how much I've been feeling sorry for myself when my life really isn't that bad. And I talked to Vanessa tonight. She misses me too."

"Of course she does," Peter said, squeezing her hand. "She's got a big heart, like her mom."

Peter finished his sandwich and then stood and stretched. "I need to get home and catch a few hours' sleep. I have to be back to the station early tomorrow, assuming there are no emergencies tonight." He rubbed a hand over his face. "I'm glad I'm not in uniform anymore; those guys are running around like crazy with all the domestic incidents."

"At Christmas?" Kate said. "You'd think people could get along at Christmas."

"Holiday time is when people absolutely *can't* get along," Peter said. "Neighbors get mad at neighbors, family feuds heat up, and parties get out of hand."

"Sounds like more reasons for me to stop feeling sorry for myself."

"Hey, your feelings are valid too," he said.

"Thanks." Kate walked him to the door and accepted a quick kiss on the cheek. As soon as he'd kissed her, a huge yawn stretched his face. In the contagious way of yawns, Kate covered a yawn of her own. "You better get home to bed. You're making me tired."

"I expect your wild day did that all by itself."

Kate rinsed out the coffee mugs and put them in the sink along with the plate and knife from Peter's sandwich. Then she wandered through the house, checking her doors and windows before heading off to bed.

The adventures of the day took their toll quickly, and Kate was soon asleep. It felt like barely minutes later when a clatter outside woke her. She sat up in bed and looked around her room, her mind still fuzzy with sleep. Moonlight shone through the open blinds on one window, making the crisp white doily on Kate's polished maple side table seem to glow.

She listened without moving, then heard more metal banging. She realized instantly what it was—her metal garbage can. When she first moved in, she'd had some trouble with a raccoon who expected a quick meal from her trash. The new cans she'd bought promised to be raccoon proof, but clearly the little bandit was inclined to test them.

Kate considered simply snuggling back under the covers, but the image of garbage strewn across her front lawn drove her out of the bed. She simply couldn't be certain the cans were raccoon proof.

She slipped on her thick blue robe and shoved her feet into a pair of slip-on canvas shoes. She didn't want to walk around outside in her slippers. She opened the front door and stuck her head out. She didn't see any trash, but the can was definitely turned over. With a sigh, Kate started across the lawn.

Suddenly a man dressed all in black, including the ski mask covering his face, stepped from around the side of the house. Kate whirled to make a run for the door, but she found the way already blocked by another masked man. She turned toward the street to make a run for Vivi's house as she opened her mouth to scream.

Fourteen

The dark shadow of Vivi's house had never looked farther away as Kate bolted across the lawn. She managed a single screech before rough hands grabbed her. A gloved hand covered her mouth as she struggled to free herself.

"Calm down," a deep voice growled in her ear. "You're coming with us."

That didn't seem like a good idea, so Kate intensified her thrashing. The big man merely lifted her off her feet. She drummed her heels against the attacker's legs, but he didn't react. He merely hauled her across the front lawn as a cargo van pulled up.

Kate spotted lights blinking on in the house directly across the street, the one beside Vivi's. The front door opened and Mrs. Rosa shuffled out onto the front stoop. "Kate?" she called into the darkness. "What's going on over there?"

Kate screamed, but the hand over her mouth made her call for help unintelligible. Still, she hoped the muffled sounds would carry over to her neighbor.

The attacker shoved her into the vehicle, and Kate tumbled onto the floor. The door slammed shut behind her, and the van lurched forward.

More hands grabbed her, this time pulling her arms behind her back and wrapping tape around her wrists. Kate heard muffled sounds and looked around. She saw Jim and Alice trussed up with tape across their mouths. Fury shone from Jim's normally sparkling blue eyes, but Alice simply looked terrified.

Rough hands slapped tape over Kate's mouth, and a hood was pulled down over her head, completely obscuring her vision. She was shoved against another seated figure, and Kate assumed it was Alice. On the hard van floor with their arms tied, they had no way to anchor themselves, and so they were frequently thrown against one another as the van drove over increasingly rough roads.

Time stretched during the uncomfortable ride. Kate suspected they were probably heading toward Eagle Mountain Lake, but they seemed to bump along for hours. Even her fear couldn't outlast the long, bumpy ride, and she was almost relieved when the van finally stopped and they were pulled out. They were shuffled a short distance through what Kate assumed was a building entranceway. A door slammed behind them.

Someone snatched off Kate's hood. She blinked against a circle of work lights strung up on metal poles and bits of scaffolding. The makeshift ring was clearly designed to make it impossible for them to make out any details beyond the circle. She turned to look at her friends just as their hoods were removed by one of the masked men.

Another masked man stepped in front of them. "Where is it?" he demanded.

Kate recognized the voice immediately. It was Edgar Henderson, the same man who had struck Jim, which meant they were almost certainly at Eagle Shipping.

"Can you be a little more specific?" Jim asked. "We know where all kinds of things are."

"You know what I'm looking for," the man growled.

"Are you after the file of photos?" Kate asked. "You

know the police have those. The detective said he showed them to you."

"I'm talking about the audio recording," Henderson said. "You had the photos; you must have the recording. I know the cops don't have that."

Kate's eyes widened, and she looked at Alice.

Jim just shook his head. "The cops *do* have it. They just can't crack MacFarlane's encryption."

The masked man seemed to consider that.

"Is that why you killed John?" Alice asked. "To get the flash drive?"

The man pointed at her. "Listen, we didn't kill anyone. *Anyone.* MacFarlane was alive when we let him go."

"Sure he was," Jim said. "And how alive do you intend to leave *us*, Mr. Henderson?"

The masked man stepped back, clearly shocked. He exchanged looks with some of the other men and then pulled off his ski mask to reveal his face. "If you try to go to the police about our little get-together tonight, I have plenty of witnesses who will be happy to place me somewhere else."

"The same witnesses who are willing to swear you didn't kill MacFarlane?" Jim asked.

"We didn't kill him!" Henderson roared. "We just brought him here to ask questions. Then we tossed his apartment."

Kate pressed her lips together. So these were the bad men who had scared John's neighbor into a heart attack. Suddenly a realization struck her. The stricken woman hadn't been saying "bad men" at all. "Battmin," she said. "The woman you scared into a heart attack said Battmin did it," Kate said.

A man near the back of the group jerked the hood from his head, and Kate saw the flushed face of Philip Battmin. He pointed at her now. "You repeat that slander anywhere, and I'll sue you for every cent you have."

"Well, lookie here," Jim said with a chuckle. "We've got the whole gang. What are you people trying to hide?"

Battmin looked them over and then shook his head. "We're not going to get anything from these people. Get them out of here."

"The way we brought them?" Henderson asked.

"I don't see any use in that. Just kick them out."

Then Battmin turned and walked outside the ring of lights. The remaining masked men quickly cut the tape binding Alice, Kate, and Jim. They herded them out of the building. As Kate had already surmised, they were at Eagle Shipping. The men marched them through the front gate and locked it behind them.

"How do we get back?" Jim shouted at them.

"Not our problem, mister," one of the men said. Then the group turned to walk back to the building, pulling off their ski masks as they left.

Kate drew her bathrobe tighter around her and shivered. The temperature might not have reached Maine lows, but it was still far too cold for an extended stay in a bathrobe and pajamas.

Jim and Alice were still wearing their day wear but no jackets. Kate cut a glance toward them. Kate recognized the thick crochet sweater Alice wore. In fact, she'd made it, but she suspected her friend wasn't any warmer in the sweater than she was in her robe. "Why aren't you in your pajamas?"

"Because they didn't grab us from our room," Alice said as she wrapped her arms around herself. "We got a call to come down to the lobby to speak to a police officer. We threw on clothes and went."

"But the only people in the lobby were our masked friends. I assume they paid off the front desk help to go be somewhere else," Jim said. "And they didn't offer to let us grab jackets before stuffing us in the van." He turned to Alice. "I left my cellphone in the room, and I assume Kate doesn't carry hers around in her robe. Please, tell me you have yours."

Alice smiled as she pulled a slim phone from her hip pocket. "Always be prepared."

"That's my little scout," he said.

Alice looked at Kate. "So do we call the police, or do you think your friend Vivi would give us a ride?"

"Knowing Vivi, she'll be disappointed if she doesn't get to ride to the rescue," Kate said. "But are you sure? It might be smart to call the police."

"Let's go for the quieter choice." Alice handed over the phone and Kate made the call.

Vivi answered the phone without a trace of sleepiness in her voice.

"I'm sorry to wake you," Kate said.

"I wasn't sleeping! I woke up to flashing lights in my window. Then Mrs. Rosa told me she saw a commotion at your house! She called the police."

"Hold on a second." Kate told Jim and Alice what Vivi had said and then turned back to the phone. "Are the police still there?"

"No. They said they didn't find any sign of violence in your house, and Mrs. Rosa didn't actually see much except moving shadows. You didn't even yell."

"I tried!" Kate yelped.

"I think the police don't pay Mrs. Rosa a lot of attention. Apparently she calls them *a lot*. And since I didn't see anything and they found nothing outside except the overturned trash can, they left."

"So, Peter didn't come."

"No. I couldn't decide if I should call him or not. I've been trying to call your phone, but it rolls to voice mail. What happened?"

"I'll tell you everything, but I need a favor," Kate said. She explained their situation and Vivi listened to the end without interrupting, though she did gasp a couple of times.

"I'll be right there," Vivi promised.

As they huddled together, the night chill made them increasingly miserable. Kate had never seen a more welcome sight than the headlights of Vivi's Mini Cooper. Kate and Alice insisted Jim take the front seat since it had the most room. Still, it took a while for them to fold him into the tiny car. Kate was near tears of gratitude when she finally slipped into the back with Alice.

Her friend cranked up the heat as soon as they piled in and then waited patiently for their teeth to stop chattering before peppering them with questions. They were almost to Sage Hills before she finally broke the silence in the car.

She glanced in the rearview, making eye contact with Kate. "Do you believe Battmin? He certainly sounds like he has a motive. He might not have pulled the trigger, but he certainly had a reason."

"Except that John's death put him in a tough spot," Kate said. "It removed the blackmailer, but they still didn't have the photos or the flash drive."

"And it doesn't make sense that they waited as long as they did to search John's apartment," Alice added. "If they knew he was dead that night, they would have beaten us and the police to John's apartment."

"But if Battmin didn't kill him," Vivi said, "who else has a motive?"

"Vasin?" Kate said dubiously.

"Which one?" Jim asked as he shifted uncomfortably in the front seat. "Him or her? My vote is on her. She's a loose cannon."

"True, and she did ask us to keep her abreast of the investigation," Alice added, "which could be her way of seeing how close we get to discovering she's the murderer."

"So, what will you be up to tomorrow?" Vivi asked. "Because you can count me in. I'm free until late afternoon. I just have to go in to prep for a small company party tomorrow night."

"There's one thing I really do think we *should* do," Kate said. "We should give Peter the flash drive."

"I agree," Alice said. "After standing out in the cold, I'll be happy to see the police figure out what Battmin is up to and throw the book at him. At *all* of them."

Kate didn't like to think of herself as a vengeful person, but she had to admit that she did want to see Battmin and the other men arrested. For one, she was really tired of being accosted. In fact, she was really tired in general. Before she knew it, Alice was gently shaking her awake. "We're at your house."

Kate woke with a start. "Right, thanks."

"Kate?" Jim asked from the front seat. "Can Alice and I crash at your house? Otherwise we'll need to call a cab to take us to the hotel."

"Oh!" Vivi yelped. "I totally didn't think of that. I should have taken you both to the hotel first. I'm sorry; it's so late, and I was just thinking about what all had happened."

"It's fine," Kate said. "Of course you can stay. The daybed in my studio has a trundle."

They thanked Vivi enthusiastically and then hauled Jim out of the front seat with considerable effort. "I haven't had this much effort put into pulling me out of something since that hotel fell on me!" he exclaimed.

Finally, they shuffled into the house. Kate pointed Alice and Jim in the direction of the studio. "If you want to shower, there are towels in the bathroom cupboard."

"In the morning," Alice said, and they disappeared down the hall.

Kate checked the windows and doors and then headed for bed herself. On the way, she decided that she didn't care if raccoons dragged her trash cans to Mexico; she was not going back outside before morning. She pulled off her robe and winced at the dirt all around the hem before she wadded it into the laundry hamper, followed by her pajama pants. Then she crawled into bed and was asleep in seconds.

After the night's horrifying events, Kate expected her dreams to be full of masked men. Instead, she found herself outside again in the cold, all alone, with her cellphone clutched in her hand. She tried to call Vivi to come and get her but she couldn't seem to make the call. She tried Peter's number, but for some reason that call wouldn't go through either. In the dream, Kate started crying as she scrolled through her contact list, calling person after person.

She woke with tears on her cheeks and shivered. She'd kicked off her covers in the night. She pulled the cozy quilt back over her and huddled for a few minutes until she felt warm again. Then she hopped out of bed and dressed quickly, careful to be as quiet as possible.

Once she was dressed, she headed for the kitchen and some lifesaving coffee, but a knock at the door stopped her midway across the living room. She froze, her heart pounding in her chest. *Stop being silly*, she scolded herself as she fought the urge to run back to her bedroom and hide. Instead, she forced herself to walk to the front door. Relief washed over her as she spotted Peter standing outside.

She threw open the door and practically flung herself into his arms. Peter held her for a moment. "Not that I'm not enjoying this," he said finally, "but are you all right? I found a police report about you on my desk this morning. One of my friends at the Sage Hills Police Department sent it over with a note that it was a false alarm. I assume from this greeting that he was wrong." His eyes narrowed. "Clearly I didn't impress on my friend how much trouble you tend to get into."

Kate eased herself away. "I'm fine, really, but it was a rough night."

He caught her by the shoulders and looked into her face. "What happened?"

"I'll tell you everything. Come in and get some coffee." She managed to hold in her questions until they got to the kitchen. "Tell me, please, did you find out anything else about Battmin Manufacturing?"

As she filled the coffee filter, Peter leaned against the counter. "The techs finally finished with the photographs," he said. "We know why those photographs were under the mattress. But I want to hear what happened to you. Where did you go last night?"

"I'll tell you, I promise, but what did you learn about the photos?"

"The secret in the photos wasn't the men or the trucks or the machines."

"Then what was it?"

"The location. One of the photos showed enough background for a tech to recognize some trees or a rock formation, some techie thing. The photos weren't taken at

Eagle Shipping. They were taken on protected land. Neither those men nor those trucks should have been on that land. I wish we knew exactly what they were doing there. The techs are working with satellite photos to match the spot exactly. Once they do, I'll head out there with a team, and we'll see if we can figure it out."

A gravelly voice said, "We might have something to help."

Peter turned to face Jim and Alice as they walked toward the kitchen. "And what would that be?" he asked.

"Hold on a second." Jim walked to the kitchen table and sat heavily. Then he unscrewed the top of his cane and fished out the flash drive. "I decided to carry this around after John's apartment was trashed." He held it out to Peter.

Peter took it and frowned. "This wouldn't be more evidence you've been withholding?"

"I'm ready to come clean as soap," Jim said, conveniently not adding that they had John's cellphone. "We haven't been able to get into the files on that. It's password protected, but I think you'll find audio files on there. Certainly Battmin thought MacFarlane had some."

Peter's eyes narrowed. "How do you know that?"

"We had a little visit from Battmin's men last night," Jim said. "All of us."

Peter turned to Kate. "That's what happened last night? Are you all right?"

Kate nodded, though she was startled by the sudden urge to cry. She blinked rapidly, then cleared her throat. "They didn't hurt us."

"Speak for yourself," Alice grumbled. "I have a nice collection of bruises from bumping around in the back of a van while tied up."

Peter's face grew darker, his eyes on Kate. "They tied you up?"

"Well, they used duct tape. It's not like it hasn't happened before." A murderer once had used duct tape to bind Kate and Vivi to the seats in Kate's van.

"Do you know most people go their whole lives without being tied up with duct tape?" Peter asked. "Just like most people actually stay out of murder investigations."

"That's what you get, friend," Jim said. "You had to fall for a Stony Point woman. Mysteries follow them like lost puppies. You might as well get used to it."

Peter pointed at Jim. "I don't need advice from you."

Jim held up his hands. "Don't shoot the messenger."

"Don't tempt me," Peter grumbled. He turned back to Kate. "Are you sure you're not hurt?"

"A few bruises, which I'm *not* going to show you," she said. "Otherwise, I'm fine. They mostly wanted to intimidate us into handing over that flash drive." She went on to tell Peter everything that had happened the night before. Several times she had to stop when her throat grew thick with the urge to cry. Peter stepped toward her once, but she held up her hand. "Let me get through it. If you hug me now, I won't make it to the end."

He nodded, but watched her with concern as she finished. "You could have called me," he said.

Kate nodded. "But I just wanted to go home. You would have had to take us to the station and ask a million questions."

"I'm not heartless," Peter answered.

"No, but you have to do your job."

Peter didn't argue with that. He looked down at the flash drive in his hand. "Well, I'll get this over to the office, and we'll pick up Battmin." He looked at Kate. "And you know Henderson was there also?"

She nodded.

"We'll pick him up too. I'm going to need witness statements from all of you."

"We'll be happy to oblige," Alice said before Jim could protest. "Shall we come down now or can we get some breakfast?"

"I'd rather you wait until I see what's on the flash drive," Peter said. "In the meantime, please stay out of trouble. These people are killers."

"Maybe they're killers," Kate said. "Battmin said that John was alive after they beat him up."

"He was hardly going to confess and then let you all go," Peter answered. "So stay away from there, and stop dragging Kate into trouble."

"We never *look* for trouble," Alice said sweetly, and Jim hooted with laughter.

"I don't want to argue," Peter said. He looked at Kate. "Battmin clearly knows where you live. Can you stay with Vivi until I get everyone picked up? And promise not to be anywhere alone?"

Kate nodded. She wasn't eager to be alone right then anyway. "I'll call Vivi. I'll be careful."

Peter gave her a quick kiss on the cheek and left without even a sip of the coffee Kate had made. She poured mugs for herself and her friends. "So, Battmin's secret had to do with being on protected land?"

"They're part of some kind of environmental group, right?" Jim asked. "That wouldn't look good. Those green people can be hostile about messing with protected land."

"The green people! Of course." Alice slapped herself lightly in the head. "Remember what Elina Vasin said? John was going to get rich, and the clue he gave her was 'green.' I guess that settles all the clues about his get-rich-quick scheme."

"But did it get him killed?" Jim asked.

Alice exhaled a long, slow breath. "I'm just happy it didn't get *us* killed. Honestly, I think I might be ready to let the police handle this. They have suspects. They aren't looking at us anymore. I think I can let it go."

"I just hope it can let us go," Kate said.

Fifteen

While Kate was cleaning up the kitchen from their break-fast, Jim and Alice took turns getting showers. When her phone rang, she glanced at the clock, wondering if it might be Vanessa calling before her day got started. It wasn't.

"Hello, Kate." The warm male voice with the touch of an accent sent a chill up Kate's spine.

"Mr. Vasin," she said hesitantly.

"Please, call me Serge. I need to speak with you and hoped you would come by my club this morning."

"I didn't think the club would be open this early."

"It isn't, but my job here begins long before the club is open. I would be honored if you could join me for lunch so I can talk with you. My chef here is quite excellent."

Kate's grip on the phone tightened as she struggled to decide the best thing to do. She certainly didn't want to be alone with Serge Vasin, though it was possible they wouldn't really be alone. If he was already there working, wouldn't others be there as well? What if he had something important to tell her related to the case? Maybe Vasin had discovered a lead.

"Kate?"

"I'm sorry, I was just thinking about my day," Kate said hesitantly. "Could you just tell me whatever you needed to say right now, over the phone?"

"It is not something I would like to say on the phone," he said. "But I assure you, it is important for you to hear."

Kate sucked on her lower lip as she struggled with the decision. "Yes," she finally blurted out, then hedged, "I should be able to come for lunch, though I may not be able to stay long."

"I will be brief then," he assured her. "So, shall we say one o'clock?"

"One o'clock. I'll be there." Kate ended the call, hoping she hadn't made a truly terrible mistake.

"Kate?"

She turned to see Alice crossing the living room, wearing the same clothes from the night before and lightly toweling her hair as she walked. "Are you all right? You look a little dazed. It's not something about Vanessa is it?"

Kate shook her head. "I just had a phone call from Serge Vasin. He wants me to come to the club for a private lunch. He said he has something to tell me."

Alice frowned. "I hope you told him no. The man strikes me as a wolf, and we're not certain he isn't also a murderer."

"I said yes. He might have discovered something about the murder. I don't think I can just ignore that. Plus, if he were the murderer, why invite just me over? I'm hardly the only one asking questions."

"If he knows something about John's murder, he could call the police."

Kate carried the phone over and dropped it into her purse. "Do you really think someone like Vasin is going to call the police?"

"I just don't think this is safe."

The soft thump of Jim's cane drew their attention across the room. Jim looked back and forth between the two of them. "You don't think what's safe?"

"Serge Vasin called Kate. He wants her to have lunch with him so he can tell her something," Alice said.

"It might be worth hearing him out," Jim said. "What restaurant is it? Alice and I could get a table nearby to keep an eye on you."

"It's at the club," Kate said.

"Which is closed during the day," Alice said. "Meaning we can't keep an eye on her. You know Peter would burst a blood vessel if you told him you were considering this."

Kate crossed her arms. "I'm not changing my mind."

"Fine, but we should get some advice from someone who actually knows this guy," Alice said.

"If you're talking about Elina Vasin, I'm really not interested in talking to her," Kate said.

Alice shook her head. "No, I'm talking about that waitress, Misty. Jim has her number. You can call her and see what she thinks. Maybe she even knows whatever it is that Vasin wants to tell you."

"She just works for the man," Kate said. "I doubt she's his best friend."

"He doesn't seem like the sort who confides in the help," Jim agreed.

Alice put her hands on her hips, not giving up. "I think she might have some worthwhile insights."

Kate thought about the idea for a moment. It seemed sensible. "Fine, I'll call her." She retrieved the phone and dialed Misty's number. The phone rang briefly before rolling to voice mail. Kate fidgeted slightly. She always felt so "on the spot" whenever she had to talk to voice mail. "Hi, Misty. This is Kate Stevens. I met you when we were asking questions about John MacFarlane. I have something else I need to ask you. If you get this call before one o'clock, please call me back."

She ended the call and dropped the phone back into her purse. "There, I tried, but she didn't answer."

"She's probably asleep," Alice said glumly. "Working so late at night, she probably sleeps until noon or later."

"That settles it," Kate said. "I'll be going to the club at one o'clock. Now I want to run over and ask Vivi about staying at her house tonight. Then I can run you guys back to your hotel."

"Fine, but only for a change of clothes," Alice said. "Other than that, we're sticking with you. We might not be able to go into the club with you, but we can stay close."

At that, a grin split Jim's face. "We can stay *really* close."

"Oh, I know that look. Your devious mind is at work. What do you mean?" Alice asked.

"We can wait in the parking lot of the club, and Kate can call one of us on her phone, then just drop it into her sweater pocket while she meets Vasin. It'll act like a wire. If we hear anything dangerous, we can charge to the rescue."

"That's a good idea," Kate said with a rush of relief. She didn't like the idea of being totally alone with Vasin any more than they did, and having them listen in and wait outside would make her feel much safer.

"Good, because I'd hate to have Peter Matthews beat me up for letting you get hurt," Jim said. "He definitely isn't happy about what happened last night."

"I'm willing to talk more about this if you want, but let's head to Vivi's first. She'll want to hear this too, and she deserves to be kept in the loop after rescuing us last night."

At Vivi's house, they settled down to mugs of her favorite beverage, a mixture of hot chocolate and coffee, and Kate brought her up to speed on her visit from Peter and the call from Vasin.

"If Peter's certain Battmin is the killer, maybe you don't need to meet with Vasin," Vivi said.

"Do you think Battmin is the killer?" Kate asked.

Vivi stirred her drink, the spoon tinkling musically against the sides of the mug. "It would be a major embarrassment for a green company to be found messing around on protected land, but it's probably one they'd weather all right. I can't see them killing over it."

"Except that we still don't know *what* they were doing on the land," Jim said. "Once the cops crack the password on the flash drive, they might discover something that's worth killing over."

"And if they do, then whatever Vasin wants to tell me will just be more icing on the cake," Kate said. "But I'm still going to be there to hear it. And I should be perfectly safe if we follow Jim's plan."

"That's assuming the call doesn't drop inside the building," Vivi said. "And assuming we can understand what's being said when the phone is in your pocket. You can't exactly hold it up in front of the man's mouth."

"It's a risk I'm willing to take," Kate said. She took a sip from her mug, wishing they would drop the subject. Her friends must have realized how nervous they were making her because Alice changed the topic by remarking on Vivi's Christmas decorations.

Vivi's face lit up. "They're all handmade. When I was a kid, my mom, my brother, and I would start making Christmas decorations in November. It was a family tradition. Mom always liked to have new things. I guess I caught the bug from her."

Alice fingered the delicate filet crochet café curtains hanging on the kitchen window. The lacy crochet depicted the nativity. "You did this?"

Vivi laughed. "Oh, no. I'd end up with a mess. No, I bought those at a Christmas bazaar. All my decorations are handmade, but only a few are from my hands."

Alice turned to look at Kate. "I bet you could do curtains like these."

Kate nodded. "I've done some filet crochet but mostly small items. In fact, my column in *Hook and Needle Artistry* this month featured filet crochet bookmarks."

"Ah, my subscription has had a terrible time trying to follow me around the country," Alice said. "I'll watch for it though. I'm not great at crochet, but I like filet. It reminds me a little of cross stitch."

They chatted some more about Alice's cross-stitch projects and Kate's crochet design work until everyone was done with their drinks. Then Kate offered to drive Alice and Jim to the hotel. "Can I come too?" Vivi asked. "I'm free until this afternoon. I can even drive, if you want."

"No," Jim begged. "I appreciate your rescue last night, but I'd really prefer not to ever cram myself into your little car again. I don't fold up so well in my old age."

Vivi laughed. "Well, I'll need to take my car and drive separately. I have to head to the hotel after your meeting with Vasin. But I definitely don't want to miss *that*."

When they reached the hotel, the group walked through the lobby toward the elevator. Kate caught Alice by the sleeve. "Vivi and I can just wait down here in the lobby while you guys change. Don't feel like you have to hurry; the furniture looks comfy."

"Good plan," Alice said. "We'll be back down soon."

Vivi and Kate sat in overstuffed chairs facing a crackling fire. The fireplace mantle held a pewter bowl full of maroon and silver ornaments and a pair of crystal candlesticks with tall maroon candles.

"The fire feels nice," Vivi said. "It's getting cold."

Kate smiled. The air outside was chillier, but her thick

sweater and light jacket had been more than warm enough. It certainly couldn't compete with a Maine Christmas chill. "I have to admit, I wouldn't mind some snow," she said. "It always feels a little more like Christmas when it snows."

Vivi wrinkled her nose. "I wouldn't get my heart set on it. We don't get snow at Christmas very often."

"What are you doing for Christmas?" Kate asked as she stretched her legs toward the fire. "Oh, wait, you told me. You're going to your mom's house."

Vivi nodded. "I'll be spending Christmas Day with Mom. Though I'll be doing something a little different from what I planned for Christmas Eve."

Something in Vivi's overly casual voice made Kate look at her with interest. "Oh?"

Vivi grinned and leaned toward Kate. "Do you remember Sam Tennyson, the Texas Ranger?"

"How could I forget?"

"Well, you know we went out a couple times," Vivi said. "And he's gorgeous, of course, but—" she wrinkled her nose, "—he's probably a little too serious for me. I think maybe he sees me as frivolous. We get along, but I don't know that we click, you know?"

Kate nodded. "I know how that is. Though I'm not sure it's fair to judge how he sees you if he hasn't said." She laughed a little. "When I first met Peter, I thought he was interested in me because he thought I was a killer."

Vivi laughed. "That's something I have trouble picturing."

"It can be easy to jump to conclusions, especially about something important. But I'm assuming you have something else to say about Sam?"

Vivi's smile brightened again. "I do. He called me to ask if I'd go to a Christmas Eve party with him. It's some family event. Honestly, I think I'm going to be there to keep his family from asking him when he's going to find a nice girl and settle down, but it should be fun. And we *do* get along really well."

Vivi shrugged, but Kate suspected she was being a little more casual about it than she actually felt. Her friend had been very interested in the handsome Ranger when they'd met him months before. "I hope you both have a wonderful time."

"I hope so too," Vivi said. "Are you and Peter doing anything for Christmas Eve?"

"I honestly don't know. I think Peter wants to, but you never know when his work will put a crimp in his plans." She sighed. "I'm feeling a little less mopey about Vanessa, but who knows how much it'll hit me on Christmas Eve? I might be horrible company."

Their chat was interrupted when Alice and Jim reappeared, looking much fresher. "We have a few hours to wait," Alice said. She turned to Vivi. "You're the one who knows the area best. What fun thing should we do to pass the time?"

Vivi tapped her cheek as she thought. "The Stockyards are always fun, but nothing really gets going there until later in the day." Then her eyes widened. "I know just the thing. One of my friends from work does some community theater, and they're doing *A Christmas Carol*. She told me there was an early matinee today."

"On Friday?" Kate said, surprised.

"What can I say? They're eager. They might not be all that good, but even bad Dickens is kind of fun." She looked at her watch. "We'd have to hurry."

They made it to the theater just moments before the show began. The building was an old church that had been converted into a theater. All the old stained glass windows were gone, filled in with boards that gave the place a slightly spooky ghost-town look. The show was charming, and hearing Dickens in a smooth Texas drawl made Kate smile. Plus, watching the play when she knew Vanessa had just watched an amateur performance of the same piece made her feel closer to her daughter. At the end, she committed anew to not letting disappointment turn her into a Christmas Scrooge.

The time spent watching the show had drained away all of Kate's jitters, but they came back with a vengeance when they walked outside and Jim said, "If you're going to meet Vasin, we'd better get over there."

Alice must have caught Kate's look of alarm. "You can still back out."

"No, I think I should do this," Kate said. "We need to hear what he knows." Just as she spoke, a fat raindrop splashed against her arm. The group hurried to their cars, but the sky opened up before they made it, and all four were a bit damp for the drive to the club.

They talked little on the drive as Kate leaned forward toward the windshield to see through the pounding rain. She parked at the back of the building, close to a big dumpster, hoping to shield her van from view of the club. Vivi slipped her Mini Cooper in beside her and waved.

Kate wrinkled her nose. "I'm not excited to walk out in that. I don't have an umbrella."

"So call and cancel," Alice suggested.

"I'll just give it a minute instead," Kate said. "Usually a rain this hard doesn't last. I shouldn't complain. We haven't had any rain at all in weeks, and I know we could use more than a quick deluge."

True to her expectation, the rain lightened in a few minutes and quit entirely soon after. Kate checked her watch and saw it was exactly one o'clock.

"Time to call my phone," Jim said.

Kate made the call and the connection seemed strong and clear. She gave her friends a slightly trembling smile. "I'll see you guys again soon. I'm sure this will be fine."

"I'm not," Alice said. "If we hear anything hinky, we're coming in."

Kate forced her hesitant steps into a confident stride as she walked around to the front of the building and entered. Even the tepid winter sun that had struggled to peek through the clouds outside left her blinded in Slammin's shadowy interior, and she stood frozen as she waited for her vision to clear.

"Kate, I am glad you came."

Kate turned toward the voice as Serge Vasin walked toward her with the same smooth stride and shark-like smile she remembered. She forced an answering smile to her lips as she hoped she hadn't just jumped in way over her head.

Sixteen

Kate smiled hesitantly at the handsome man in the perfectly tailored suit. "You said you had something to tell me?"

"I do, but come and join me for lunch. We do not need to blurt secrets at one another in the doorway like spies in a bad movie." He guided her toward a table with his hand in the small of her back. Kate resisted the urge to flinch away from him.

Compared with Kate's two previous visits, far more lights were on in the club as they walked through, and the music that played quietly in the background was more romantic, with no pounding dance beat.

The table had been set up in the middle of the dance floor, clearly placed there specifically for their lunch. It was a small round table with a crisp white tablecloth and two chairs. Vasin pulled out Kate's chair, and she slipped into it.

Vasin sat down in his chair, which Kate found uncomfortably close to her own. "You looked lovely when last I saw you, but I like this Kate better."

"That dress was more like a costume," Kate said as she considered scooting her chair away slightly. "I was trying to blend in."

"Even in that dress, you stood out like a flower in the snow." Vasin leaned toward her and his leg brushed hers. Kate scooted her chair slightly to give them more room.

"You're very kind. Did you have something to tell me about John MacFarlane's death?"

"As I said before, I have little interest in John MacFarlane."

Kate looked at him sharply. "Then I'm confused. You said you had something to tell me?"

He nodded. "I do, but it is not about that man or his death."

"Then what?"

Vasin held up a hand to signal a pause as a server walked up with a bottle of wine. "You should have some of this, Kate. It is quite exquisite."

Kate shook her head, placing a hand over the glass on the table. "No thank you. Water will be fine for me."

"Such a Puritan," Vasin said. "Do you ever let yourself have fun?"

"I do, but it doesn't usually involve wine, especially not with a man I barely know."

"Is not that the best part of any relationship? The getting to know?"

Kate sat back in her chair and stared at him, completely confused. "No, I don't really think that's true," she said finally. "I think the best part of a relationship is when two people really understand and trust each other. Then time together is more valuable, more honest."

"Do you think I am dishonest?"

"I don't think a lot about it," Kate said. She gestured around the room. "Your life is certainly very different from mine."

"But is that not the saying? Opposites attract?"

"Mr. Vasin—"

"Serge."

"Serge …" She smiled tightly. "I'm not entirely sure why I'm here. I came because I thought you had something to tell me about John's death."

"Did I say this?"

Kate shook her head. "No, but I had certainly made my interest in John's murder pretty clear."

Vasin reached across and took Kate's hand from where it rested on the edge of the table. "And I wish to make my interest very clear, but my interest is not about that detestable man."

"Oh. I thought I told you I'm seeing someone." Kate tried to ease her hand away, but Vasin's grip on her fingers was firm, though not tight enough to be painful. She didn't want to turn it into an arm wrestling match, so she sat still.

"I am not someone who lets the existence of competition keep me from pursuing what I want."

Kate looked into his eyes and felt a chill at the intensity of his focus on her. Once again she had the feeling of sharing space with a predator, and she was afraid she might have passed too close to the lion's den this time. She wasn't entirely sure what to say next, but she decided to go with honesty. *Here's hoping it really is the best policy.* "You're a very interesting man. And I am flattered by your attention, but I'm not interested in a relationship with you. I'm seeing someone. I'm not the kind of woman who dumps a man just because someone else shows an interest."

"This man you are seeing, he leaves you to go to clubs without him. He leaves you to eat alone. What kind of relationship is this?"

"The kind I like." Kate stood up. "I'm sorry. I'm sure you had a lovely lunch planned, but I don't want to give you any false impressions." She smiled a little. "I went through a 'bad boy' phase many years ago. I even married one. But I'm looking for something very different now."

Vasin stood smoothly, looking down at her. "You think I am bad."

"I think you can be."

"I can also be good." He smiled though it did little to warm his features. "You would be a good influence on me, Kate."

She smiled. "I don't want to be an influence. I don't want that kind of uncertainty or work."

He nodded. "You are an honest woman. I am not used to being spoken to thus. I wish you felt differently."

"But I don't."

"Are you certain you do not want to stay for lunch? I promise to behave."

"No, thank you. I actually should go and meet my friends."

"Then let me walk you to the door." He turned to lead her through the club, but not in the direction of the front door.

"Where are we going?"

"Are you not parked in back of the club? One of my men observed you park your van near the dumpster. A most unpleasant spot, but it would be easier if you leave through a door closer to your van, no?"

"Yes, that would be fine." Kate was hesitantly grateful that he'd reacted so calmly to what she said. She still felt tense all over as she followed Vasin through the shadowy club, not ready to relax completely until she was out of the building.

At the door, Vasin again took her hand. He smiled into her eyes. "I would try to change your mind, but I think it would only make you like me less."

"Probably," Kate said.

"Then I let you go." He released her hand and nodded as one of the night bouncers opened the heavy rear door for her. "But you are always welcome at my club."

"Thank you." Kate fought down the urge to run through the door and instead walked out at her normal pace. As the door closed behind her, she felt a surge of relief so strong it made her knees feel weak.

Kate slipped her hand into her jacket pocket and slipped out her phone. She held it up to her ear. "You heard?"

Alice's voice was a welcome sound in her ear. "Yes. You'll be happy to know that I kept Jim from running inside a couple of times to rescue you."

As Kate walked across the parking lot, she smiled at the mental image. Then she heard an odd bang, followed immediately by the sound of an object striking the door to the club behind her. "What was that?"

Another bang rang out, and this time Kate recognized it for what it was as something brushed the sleeve of her thick crochet jacket. Someone was shooting at her!

Kate threw herself down to the pavement, then army-crawled quickly behind a posh sports car parked nearby. She tugged at the sleeve of her jacket, pulling it so she could see it better. A ragged tear showed severed stitches across the upper bicep of the sleeve. Not only was someone shooting at her, but the person had nearly hit her!

The roar of an engine and the screech of tires made Kate jump as Alice raced the van over to stop on the other side of the sport car, offering another layer of protection between Kate and the shooter. "Are you all right?" Alice called through the driver's window.

Kate nodded. "Someone shot at me!"

"I know. I heard."

Kate looked around in a panic. "Where's Vivi? Is she all right?"

"She's fine," Alice said. "She had to leave for work as soon as your lunch was wrapping up."

The back door to the club flew open and two big bouncers raced out, followed by Vasin. They men seemed intent on acting as a wall between Vasin and the possible shooter, but he waved them away and continued toward Kate. He reached her side in moments. "Are you hurt?"

Kate was still squatting behind the sports car. "No, I'm all right."

He looked at Kate's van and then pointed at his men. "Get Kate safely into the van. At once."

One of the big men reached down and hauled Kate to her feet, keeping her body shielded with his own. He towed her toward the rear door of the van.

"I think the shooter left," Kate said.

Vasin turned from scanning the parking lot to look directly at her, his gaze sharp. "I will not take that risk."

"We'd rather not take that risk either," Alice agreed.

One of the two big men opened the van door and the other practically threw Kate inside. Vasin walked over to look into the window. "I will discover who tried to hurt you on my property. This person will not do so again."

Kate shivered at the menace in the man's voice. "Don't worry about me."

"I do not waste energy in worry."

That didn't make her feel better.

Vasin looked pointedly at Alice. "You must take Kate to safety."

"We're going now," Alice said. "Thanks for getting Kate safely to the car."

The van rumbled and bounced across the parking lot and, Kate hoped, away from the shooter. *Someone tried to kill me*, Kate thought weakly. *What am I going to do now?*

Alice pulled out of the club lot and drove west. Kate leaned back against the seat and thought about how much she wasn't cut out for the action-hero life.

"Peter is going to freak out," she said.

"That's likely to be a mild version of his response," Jim said. "And it'll probably start when he hears you met Vasin for lunch and just go up from there."

Kate nodded. "You're probably right." She closed her eyes for a moment and then opened them again. "Do you think we could stop somewhere? I'm feeling a little nauseated."

"I'm surprised you're not feeling totally hysterical," Alice said. She pulled into the lot of the first diner they came upon, and the trio climbed out of the van. Alice took one look at Kate and put an arm around her. "Feeling shaky?"

"A little."

They headed into the diner and took a corner booth. Kate ordered a ginger ale, hoping the carbonation would settle her stomach. "That was officially the worst lunch date I've ever had," she said softly.

Alice laughed at that. "And I thought it was intense *before* the shooting started. Are you sure you're all right?"

Kate nodded, but she tugged her sleeve to show the damage to Alice. "I loved this jacket! I'll have to put on two new sleeves and use a contrasting color or maybe something variegated. There's no way I can get the color to match if I just replace this one."

A bark of laughter drew their attention. "I like that your response to having a bullet hole in your jacket is how you can best repair it," Jim said.

"This is one of my favorite jackets!" Kate protested.

"I'm not criticizing," Jim said. "I just think you're made of tougher stuff than you let on."

Kate thought about that. Her stomach was still upset and her hands were trembling when she picked up her soda. "I don't know about tough. I was terrified. I still am. Why would someone shoot at *me*?"

"That's an excellent question," Alice replied. "I'd like the answer to that myself."

Jim leaned back and laid an arm across the back of the

booth. "What if it was Vasin? Having someone shoot at Kate might have been his way of looking like a hero who comes to the rescue."

Kate gaped at him. "That's crazy."

Jim raised a shoulder in a half-shrug. "The man strikes me as quite capable of crazy."

"But the bullet nearly hit me."

"Yeah, that's a little extreme," Alice agreed. "Maybe it was Vasin's sister. She already tried to warn you away from her brother. Maybe this is her getting serious."

"That would go a long way toward explaining why Kate would be a target for anyone," Jim said. "All of us together have been investigating John's murder. Why pick on Kate? But crazy Elina might be an explanation."

"I think we're still missing a piece to this puzzle," Kate said. "The question is, where do we find it?"

"I think we need to go back to the beginning again," Alice said.

"You mean John's apartment?" Kate felt a flutter of worry. *Peter will love that.* Of course, he might be so distracted by the fact that Kate was nearly shot that he wouldn't even notice the whole breaking-and-entering thing—again. "Maybe I should call Peter."

"And say what?" Jim asked curiously.

"Well, I did just get shot at."

Alice caught Kate's eye. "By someone we never saw, shooting a gun we didn't recover any bullets from, beside a club that Peter will be thrilled that you returned to."

"Peter might find the bullet," Kate said. "He'd probably bring his team to the club with him."

"Assuming Serge didn't already take care of that." Alice drummed on the pitted tabletop nervously. "You probably should call him. We'll wait to decide what to do next after you talk to him."

Kate nervously dialed Peter's number. He picked up immediately. "Kate, I'm going into an interrogation. Is this something that can wait?"

I should say no. I really should. I should tell him now. "It can wait," Kate said. "I'll talk to you later."

"OK, later."

Kate looked sheepishly at her friends. "He was on the way to an interrogation."

"And you chickened out," Jim said.

"A little bit." Kate sighed. "We can go to John's apartment. How much more trouble can we possibly get into?"

"Oh, darlin'," Jim said, "don't say that."

"Too late," Alice said, grinning. "The gauntlet has been thrown. Let's go see how much more trouble we can get into."

Seventeen

The hallway of the apartment building was cool and slightly shadowy. As they passed through the hall, Kate glanced at Esther Winn's apartment door and wondered how the older woman was doing. It seemed like no one John MacFarlane had ever met went undamaged.

Kate's attention was pulled ahead to the end of the hall as Jim tapped on John's door, mostly for display, and then took two long, slender tools from his jacket pocket and set about picking the lock, ignoring the police tape across the door.

As they walked into the still-littered apartment, Kate asked, "What are we looking for?"

"I think our greatest need right now is to get into John's phone," Alice said. "He was never good at remembering things like that—passwords, pin numbers, my birthday. So, he either picked something he couldn't forget or he kept a reminder around."

"And you tried all the likely things you knew about," Jim said.

"Right. But it's been years since I was around John, so there could be something obvious that I'm missing," Alice said as her gaze swept the room. "I'm still thinking the clue is here."

Kate walked into the kitchenette. The floor was littered with slips of paper from John's "positive affirmation" kick. Someone had swept the papers and magnets onto the floor. Kate nudged a pile of them, and they slipped apart like dry leaves. "I wonder if the password could be related to any of these. With so many stuck around the place, he could have put the password right out in plain sight, and no one would think of it."

"*You* did," Jim said. "But there's nothing better than hiding in plain sight."

"We can try a word from every slip," Alice said. As Alice and Jim gathered up the papers from the kitchen floor, Kate walked to the bathroom and brought back the notes from the mirror.

While Kate was in the bathroom, Alice had pulled out the phone and had begun typing in main words from each of the slips of paper: "winner," "success," "challenge," "determination." Nothing unlocked the phone.

"How about something obvious?" Jim asked. "Like 'positive' and 'affirmation.' Give those a try."

Alice typed in the words, but still the phone wouldn't unlock.

"It was a good guess," Jim said.

Kate walked out into the dining area. The floor there was littered with pages ripped from the book that had been on the table. "How about this book?" She picked up a ragged piece torn from the cover. "This book was right out in the open. Maybe he used something from it?"

They quickly picked up all the cover bits they could find and tried different words, including the author's name. Kate felt a stir of hope as Alice carefully typed in "Ogilvie," but still no luck.

Jim leafed through torn pages, and Alice tried words from sections that John had underlined or where he had made margin notes. Nothing unlocked the phone.

"Maybe I'm wrong," Alice said. "Maybe the clue isn't here in the apartment at all."

"Don't give up so easily, Red," Jim said as he limped into

the living area. Clumps of pillow stuffing lay around the room like snowballs.

As Kate walked to the middle of the seating area, the bits of glass left from the broken photo frame they'd seen days before crackled under her feet. She looked for the photo and saw that it had been torn into several pieces.

"Maybe we should check the bedroom," Alice said to Jim. "You did find the folder in there, so we know John used it as a hiding place."

"Sounds good to me," Jim said.

Kate didn't look up from the floor. Instead, she collected the pieces of photo while Jim followed Alice into the bedroom. One strip held most of John's face; his grin looked even cockier when seen in such a focused glimpse. Another strip held his folded arms. More strips revealed bits of the car. Kate continued to search the floor although there was no particular reason why she thought the photo might be important.

When she'd collected all of the pieces, she carried them over to the dining table and laid them out in jumbled order. She flipped each strip over, thinking perhaps John had written the password on the back of the photo, but the backs were blank.

She still felt the nagging sense that something was on the photo, so she began to reassemble the pieces into the picture. *Why would someone have a photo of himself?* Sure, everything she knew about John MacFarlane revealed a tendency toward narcissism, but why was this the only photo in the whole apartment? Something had to be special about it.

Kate gazed down at the finished photo. As before, John leaned against the beautiful dove-gray Jaguar. John's blue suit contrasted nicely with the soft gray. His arms were crossed over his chest, and he had one leg casually crossed over the other at the ankle. Kate considered the pose. What if the password was something like "crossed"? She wrinkled her nose. That seemed a little silly.

Suddenly Kate's eyes widened. "Alice! Jim! What about the car?"

Her friends came out into the room. "What car?"

Kate tapped the photo. "This Jaguar. He had his picture taken with it. It must be his car. Maybe there are clues in it. Has anyone searched the car?"

Alice's eyes gleamed with interest. "Did Peter mention a car?"

Kate shook her head.

Alice and Jim exchanged glances. "That Jaguar does seem like a good possibility. Since John was hustled out by Battmin's men, the Jag is probably outside somewhere."

Alice gave Jim a mischievous grin. "How good are you at picking car locks?"

"Not as good as apartments," Jim said. "Especially something high-end like that. It will probably be alarmed. But we could look in the windows and get Kate's boyfriend to check out the car."

They walked out to the parking lot and looked around. No dove-gray Jaguar was parked in any of the spaces. As they walked from car to car, a man in a robe stepped out on one of the apartment balconies and called down. "Can I help you?"

Alice turned a smile toward the man. "We're looking for John MacFarlane's Jaguar."

"John MacFarlane?" No sign of recognition registered on the man's face.

"He was your downstairs neighbor. He had an apartment on the first floor of your building," Alice called.

Jim chimed in helpfully. "Tall guy. Dark hair. Slick. Looked like an insurance salesman." Alice gave him an elbow lightly in the ribs.

"Oh, yeah, I remember him," the man said. "He doesn't own a Jaguar. His car is that little red Toyota." He pointed toward a car near the entrance of the building.

"Are you sure?" Kate asked.

The man nodded. "I've seen him washing it at the apartment's car wash. Is this guy a friend of yours?"

"An ex," Alice said.

"You have my condolences," the man said. "He seemed like a jerk."

"He was," Jim called. "Thanks for your help."

They walked slowly back to the apartment. "Why would John have a photo of a Jaguar when he owns a Toyota?" Kate asked.

"Wishful thinking?" Jim asked. Then his eyes lit up. "Or a clue. You want to try the word 'Jaguar'?"

Alice punched it into the phone but still got nothing. She sighed and stared down at Kate's reassembled photo on the apartment's dining table. "Maybe. I wonder whose car it is."

"A really wealthy friend?" Kate asked.

"And who do we know who fits that description?" Alice asked. She pulled out her phone and punched in a number.

"Who are you calling?" Jim asked.

"Hello, Miss Vasin?" Alice asked. "This is Alice MacFarlane. I have a quick question to ask you. It might sound odd. Do you own a gray Jaguar?" She gave Jim and Kate a wide-eyed look. "You do! Do you know why John had his photo taken in front of your car?" Jim and Kate fidgeted nervously as Alice nodded while listening. Finally, Alice said, "The photo? He had it in a frame in his apartment." Another pause. "I'm sorry. I can't. When someone trashed John's apartment, they tore it up. I just happened to remember it, and since I knew John didn't own a car like that …" She paused again and listened for a while longer. Then she thanked the woman and ended the call.

"I don't suppose she said anything about shooting at me?" Kate said.

"It didn't come up. You want me to call her back?" Alice asked.

"Let's stay on task," Jim insisted. "What did she say?"

"Elina said John was obsessed with the Jaguar, and she sometimes let him drive it, though he hadn't driven it for weeks. She assumed he had his photo taken with it so he could pretend it was his. She asked me to bring it to her so she could burn it."

"A weird thing to ask for," Jim said.

"She's a weird woman," Alice said. "I still think she's disappointed that she didn't get to torture John to death."

"Charming thought," Jim remarked.

Kate turned to look down at the torn photo, struggling to let go of her worry about the shooting and focus on the clue in front of her. The Jaguar was beautiful. She supposed she could see why he'd want one. But was he so obsessed with the car that he wanted to look at the photo all the time?

"Why frame this photo?" Kate asked. "It's the only photo in the whole apartment."

"It might be like the positive affirmations," Jim said. "It was his way of keeping his eyes on the prize. He wanted to be rich enough to buy one of his own. That fits with all those pieces of paper."

"True, but isn't that all the more reason why his password might come from it?" Kate said. Then she drew in a small sharp breath and pointed at the photo. "What about the license plate? Wouldn't that be a great password?"

Alice quickly typed in the plate number and then whooped as the phone unlocked. "Kate, you're a genius!"

Kate felt the warmth on her cheeks that always signaled a blush. "I'm just glad it worked."

Alice flipped through John's contact list, but it didn't produce any useful surprises.

"Try his texts," Jim said. "Who were the last people he communicated with?"

Alice messed with the phone for a moment and then gasped. She held up the phone with the screen pointing toward them. "This was his last text from the night he died."

The message was simple: "Battmin's men coming. Find me." The recipient's name was a surprise: Misty Rayne.

"Interesting that Miss Rayne didn't tell us about this message when we talked to her," Jim said.

"Perhaps we should chat with her again," Alice said.

"I left that voice mail. She hasn't called back," Kate said. "Do we wait until she calls?"

Jim headed for the door. "Not hardly. Let's go visit Miss Rayne."

They were surprisingly quiet on the drive over. Kate didn't know about her friends, but she hated to think of the struggling single mother having anything to do with John's death. After being raised by a single mother and then struggling through her own single-mother years after her divorce, Kate related strongly to the young woman's situation.

When they reached the apartments, Alice slipped into the closest parking space and asked, "What's the game plan?"

"The direct assault," Jim said.

"But not too rough," Kate insisted. "We don't know that she doesn't have a good reason for not telling us about the message."

"I'm sure she does," Jim answered. "Namely that it would have solved the murder a long time ago."

Kate shook her head. "I don't know. She's just a single mom raising her child as best she knows how. She got involved with the wrong guy, but why kill him?"

Jim turned in his seat and gave Kate a grim smile. "That's one of the many questions I'd like to ask her."

"Just be nice. Please?"

Jim held her gaze for a moment and then huffed. "Fine. Direct but nice."

Alice reached out and squeezed his arm. "That's my tough guy."

When they reached the door, Kate stepped forward and knocked politely before Jim had a chance to pound on it. They stood quietly, but no one answered. Then Jim stepped up and rapped on the door with his cane.

The door cracked open a minute later. They saw Misty's face in the crack behind the door chain. She blinked at them. "What do you want?"

"We want to talk about the message John left for you on the night he was murdered," Jim said.

She narrowed her eyes. "You woke me for that?"

"Please, Miss Rayne," Kate said. "It's important."

Misty sighed noisily and then undid the chain and let them in. The front room of the apartment was shadowy. Kate looked around, noticing the lack of Christmas decorations. "Your daughter isn't here?"

"Mom takes her so I can sleep," Misty said pointedly. "I work nights, remember?"

"The last time we were here, you said your daughter was Christmas shopping with your mom," Kate said. "But you still don't have any Christmas decorations up."

"My mom does that stuff," Misty said. "I don't have the room or the time. Are you here to critique my decor?"

"No."

"We came because we have John's phone," Jim said. "We know he sent you a text on the night he died. A text saying Battmin's men were coming for him and that he needed you."

Misty nodded. "I didn't get that text. My phone was off at the time, and when I turned it back on ..." She shrugged. "I really didn't care what he needed. He was a two-timing jerk."

"So, you didn't drive out to Eagle Mountain Lake?" Alice asked.

Misty shook her head. "Never been there. I work late; then I come home and sleep. Which is, by the way, what I was doing when you banged on my door."

Kate's gaze continued to roam the room around them. She thought how sad it was that Misty didn't have a single Christmas decoration. What she'd said about her mom made sense, but that also seemed like giving up. Part of being a mom was making Christmas special for your child. She thought of how hard she'd worked to be sure Vanessa had a good Christmas after the divorce even though money was painfully tight.

Suddenly Kate's eyes stopped near the front door. She saw damp indentations in a small rug and a pair of soaked canvas shoes. She quickly pulled her gaze back to Misty. "What time do you get home in the morning?"

"Usually about four," Misty said. "It depends on whether the boss needs us for a private party."

"Did that happen this morning?" she asked.

"Actually, yeah, we had to do some setting up this morning early, though it wasn't for anything big. Apparently the boss was going to entertain a lady at the club." She shrugged.

"It's happened before. At any rate, I've been home since early this morning."

"Home sleeping?"

Misty frowned. "Mostly."

"You didn't go out?"

"No."

"That's interesting," Kate said. "Because apparently your shoes did." She pointed at the shoes on the rug. "And I think I know why. You shot at me!"

Eighteen

Misty glared at her. "What are you talking about? Are you crazy?"

"Your shoes were out in the hard rain, and that happened only a little while ago. Why would your shoes go out without you?"

Misty narrowed her eyes. "I wasn't out. I just washed my shoes."

"Really?" Kate walked over to the shoes. Misty tried to head her off, but Jim got in her way. Kate picked up a shoe and looked at it. "You didn't do a very good job. These shoes are still dirty."

"So I'm not a great cleaner."

Kate ran a finger across the sole and it came away black. "This is dirt that would have come off if you'd rinsed the shoe enough to account for how wet it is. You didn't wash these; you wore them out in the rain." She stared at the young woman, completely astounded. "You were at the club, weren't you? But I don't understand. Why shoot at me?"

Misty crossed her arms over her chest. "I don't know what you're talking about."

"Why would you shoot at *me*?" Kate squeaked. She knew she was repeating herself, but she was desperate for an answer.

"Fine," Misty said, dropping her arms. She snatched a pack of cigarettes from a table and lit one. "I shot at you. I missed, didn't I?"

"Barely!" Kate yelped.

Jim limped over to crowd Misty's personal space. "Miss Rayne, I don't actually like it when people shoot at my friends. I think you need to explain yourself."

Misty backed up and bumped against the table behind her. She bent to look around Jim at Kate. "I got your text message just as I got home this morning. I didn't think that much about it. I just wanted to get to bed. It had been a long night, and I helped set up like I said."

"Go on," Jim growled.

"I was getting ready for bed when I realized I'd left my new hat at the club." She smiled a little. "My daughter bought it when she was out shopping with my mom. She's still too young to wait until Christmas when she has a surprise. I only wore the hat to work because she insisted. I couldn't wear it to wait on customers. Vasin is a stickler about the uniform. I'm not used to having a hat, so I accidentally left it behind, but I didn't want to risk someone stealing it. It's happened before."

"So you went back," Alice said encouragingly.

Misty nodded. "I did." She turned her gaze back to Kate. "I got there just in time to see you go in. I realized you were the lady friend we'd set up for, but you were asking all these questions about John. I thought you were working with Vasin somehow; maybe looking for John's killer on account of Elina having a thing for him too. I thought crazy Elina might kill me if she found out I was one of the women he'd cheated on her with."

"So you *shot* at me?" Kate said.

"I lost my head. I just panicked. I keep a gun in my car because of all the creeps I have to deal with at work. Sometimes they wait for me in the parking lot. It's good to have some way to scare them off, so I keep pepper spray in my uniform pocket and a gun in the car."

"I can't believe you tried to kill me."

"I didn't," Misty insisted. "I just wanted to scare you away. I figured you might blame Vasin for the shooting. I heard people he works with get shot sometimes. And if you were scared of Vasin, you wouldn't want to work with him anymore. At any rate, a shooting would distract everyone."

"But you almost hit me! And you ruined my favorite jacket."

Misty gave a wobbly, apologetic smile. "Yeah, a handgun isn't very accurate at any distance. I didn't mean to shoot so close. I thought maybe I hit you. I panicked and ran. I came straight home."

"So, the gun you shot at Kate with," Jim said. "Is that the same gun you used to murder John?"

"I told you, I didn't murder him! I didn't!"

"Then you won't mind turning the gun over to the police," Alice said, "so they can compare it to the bullet that killed John."

"I'd rather not," Misty said. "I don't want to get in trouble."

"That ship sailed when you shot at our friend." Jim pulled out his phone. "We'll just call the police and let them sort this out."

Misty leaned against the table behind her and then quickly opened a small drawer and pulled out a snub-nosed revolver. "No one is calling the police!"

Jim held out both hands to Misty. "You don't want to hurt anyone else."

The gun never wavered in her hand. "I don't, but I also don't want to go to prison, so you stay back. I'm getting out of here."

"And then what?" Kate asked. "Run? Keep running? What about your daughter?"

Misty raised her chin. "My mom will take care of her."

Kate walked over to the television stand and picked up the framed photo of Misty and her daughter. "And then what?

This becomes the only memory she has of you? You're just the mom who ran off and left her?"

"And how would it be better if I'm the mom who ends up in prison?"

"That's not ideal, but it's better than nothing," Kate insisted. "Doesn't she deserve that? From what you said, it sounds like she loves you. Don't throw that away."

Misty blinked wet eyes at Kate. "I don't know what to do."

"Just give us the gun and tell us what happened," Kate said gently.

Misty looked down at the gun in her hand then back up at Kate. Conflict showed starkly on her face. Finally she shook her head. "I can't." She turned and ran for the door, but Jim thrust out his cane and Misty tumbled over it. She hit the floor hard and the gun went off. The screen of the television next to Kate seemed to explode.

Alice lunged for the gun, but all the fight had gone out of Misty Rayne. She covered her eyes to weep.

Kate stared at the television. "I'm really getting tired of being shot at today!"

Jim offered her a crooked smile. "Sorry. It seemed like the right thing to do at the time."

Alice and Kate gently hauled Misty to her feet as Jim dialed Peter's number. Misty seemed barely able to stand, so they helped her to a slightly ratty overstuffed chair. Kate sat on the edge of a coffee table nearby and took Misty's hands in her own. "Do you want to tell us what really happened when John called you?"

Misty looked at Kate, her face a mask of misery. "I knew about the other women already. He'd told me they didn't mean anything to him. They were just a means to an end, especially Elina. He said he loved me."

"He said that a lot," Alice said.

Misty looked up at her silently for a moment and then nodded. "I know. Now."

"So, you thought he loved you," Kate said, pulling her attention back to the night of John's death. "And that's why you went looking for him when he texted you."

She nodded. "It was late, and I was tired. I'd just gotten off work. I wasn't even home yet when the message came in." She looked between the two women. "You saw the message? He called me like a dog, and I came."

"You saw something in him that wasn't there," Alice said.

Misty nodded. "I drove out to Battmin Manufacturing, but I didn't see anything going on, so I tried Eagle Shipping. That's when I found John limping down the road. He looked terrible. His nose had been bleeding, and one eye was swollen. I wanted to take him to the hospital."

"Why didn't you?"

"He didn't want to go. He was so angry. He kept saying that no one could treat him like that. I didn't even know why someone beat him up. He wouldn't say, but I knew he had some kind of business with Battmin. He told me once that Battmin was going to make him rich."

"It would have saved a lot of time if you'd told us about John's connection to Battmin when we first met," Alice said.

"I was just trying to keep from being connected with that night." Misty wiped her eyes with the heels of her hands. "John demanded I give him my gun."

"Why did he want your gun?" Alice asked.

"He was ranting again, saying no one could treat him like that. I didn't want him to have my gun. That gun is registered to me. If he shot someone, it would come back on me. So I told him he couldn't have it."

"That's reasonable," Alice said.

Misty nodded eagerly. "But he wasn't being reasonable. He shoved me out of the way and went after the gun in my car. He said he was going to take it and take my car. He said he'd come back and pick me up as soon as he could." She looked at them, her face still mirroring the shock from that suggestion. "He was going to leave me out there in the middle of nowhere. I didn't even have a coat on."

"What did you do?"

"I told him he couldn't have my car or my gun," Misty said. "And I said he wouldn't even have suggested it if he loved me."

Her face seemingly crumbled, and she cried softly for a moment.

"He didn't love you," Alice said, her voice barely above a whisper.

"No. He laughed at that. He called me a …" She stopped, unable to spit out the word. Kate could feel the pain radiating from her trembling body. Harry had called her plenty of rude names when he was drinking and angry. She knew how much they hurt, especially when you so desperately wanted to believe that the man saying them loved you.

"How did John get shot?" Jim asked simply.

"He took the gun out of my glove compartment. I couldn't let him have it. I grabbed for it, and we wrestled over it. Normally he would have taken it from me easily; he was a lot bigger. But he'd been beaten up. Finally, I thought I had the gun, and then … it just went off."

"And the bullet hit John in the chest," Alice said.

Misty nodded. "I had to get him to the hospital. We were right there at the car. He sort of crumpled, and I managed to shove him into the seat. I keep a towel in the backseat in case my daughter spills something. I used that to try to stop the bleeding, but he was bleeding so much. Still, I thought he'd be all right as soon as I got him to the hospital."

"But he wasn't," Alice said.

"No. When I ran around the car and got in the driver's seat, he'd already stopped moaning. I called his name over and over. He didn't answer. And I could see in the car light that he wasn't breathing. He died so fast."

"He took a bullet to the chest," Jim said.

"I didn't know what to do. I hadn't meant to hurt him, but it was my gun. And everyone knew he'd cheated on me. *I* knew he'd cheated on me. Who would believe he died accidentally?"

"So, you got rid of the body," Jim prompted.

"We were pretty close to the lake. I knew the area from when I was a kid. I figured I'd just put him in the lake. So, I drove up to the spot where my dad used to fish. I knew I could get the car close there. And I dragged John's body out of my car and pushed him into the water. I was going to tow him out deeper into the lake, but someone yelled at me. I panicked and ran off."

"The person who yelled at you is probably the one who called the police about a body," Kate said.

"I really didn't mean to kill him," Misty whispered.

The women all jumped at the sound of sirens approaching. Misty looked at them with frightened eyes. "What's going to happen now?"

"Now you're going to tell your story again," Kate said, taking the woman's hand. "You tell the truth for yourself and your daughter. The detective coming is a good man. You'll be all right." She hoped what she was saying was true, but she suspected nothing would be all right for Misty Rayne for a long time.

Nineteen

When Kate met Peter at her house after church on Sunday, she paused in the front room to gaze at the rather sad, bare Christmas tree. Peter stepped behind her and gave her a hug. "We'll decorate today. It'll be beautiful."

She turned to smile at him. "Are you sure you can spare the time?"

"Well, Misty confessed, and the investigation into Battmin has been handed over to a different department. No one connected with the businesses was involved in John's death."

Kate walked to the kitchen to get them something to eat with Peter following. "They just worked illegally on protected land," she said.

"They did a little more than that. That password you figured out worked on the flash drive too, and we discovered a tidy collection of sound files. Apparently Battmin was dumping out there and using Eagle Shipping to move the waste."

Kate turned to look at Peter. "Not very green of them."

"Not by a long shot. They'll have all kinds of fines to pay, but the public relations toll is liable to be much, much bigger."

"Big enough to commit murder?" Kate asked.

"Maybe, but not in this case. We know who actually killed John."

Kate sighed as she turned to the coffeemaker. "I can't help but feel bad for Misty. I know what it's like to want so badly to believe in someone."

Peter put his arms around her waist. "You're a special lady."

She turned to look at him suspiciously. "Why? Anyone would feel for her. She has a little girl who loves her."

"She also shot at you," Peter said. "And nearly hit you."

"I guess people do desperate things when they're scared," Kate said. "It doesn't change how I feel about the situation that got her into this mess in the first place. I know what it's like to invest emotionally in a man who doesn't really feel the same way."

Peter sighed and ran a hand through his hair. "You know all men aren't like that, right?"

She smiled. "Looking for a compliment, detective?"

"No, just checking to be sure you weren't painting all of us with the same brush. I know you and Alice both have been through a lot. But look at Alice and Jim. They're making it work."

Kate laughed. "They just raced around Fort Worth trying to prove they weren't murderers so they could get married. That seems an extreme way to make it work."

"A guy does what he can." Peter leaned back against the counter as Kate handed him a mug of coffee. "So, when are they getting married?"

"I'm not sure. Alice said they're having a recuperation day today, and then they're tackling the wedding stuff tomorrow. I'm sure they'll let me know when it's going to happen. I *am* supposed to be there."

He smiled at her and reached out to tug a strand of hair away from her face. "You should wear flowers in your hair. That would look real pretty."

Kate shook her head. "It's not my wedding. I imagine I'll just wear a dress and look respectable."

"You do a fine job at respectable," Peter said. "Now, can

we have a sandwich before I starve?"

After lunch, they spent a cheerful hour decorating the Christmas tree and sipping the eggnog Kate surprised Peter with. "I wanted to be properly prepared when we got around to decorating again," she explained.

Decorating would have taken longer, but Peter finally gave in on his ban on tinsel flinging, though he called Kate a barbarian with each toss.

As Kate hung ornaments, she paused often to tell Peter the story behind each decoration. Peter listened attentively to the entire Christmas story. Kate finished with the tale of the rather bug-eyed, three-legged lamb ornament Vanessa made when she was little. "I'm probably boring you to death with all this talk about the decorations."

"Not at all. You don't talk a lot about yourself or the past, so I'm getting a little peek with each ornament." He smiled and gently poked the lamb, sending it swinging. "Honestly, it's helping me understand why we have a zombie sheep on our Christmas tree."

"It's not a zombie sheep!" Kate said. Then she peered closer at the little ornament. "It does look a little like a zombie sheep."

"I rest my case."

A perky ringtone drew a smile from Kate, and she hurried across the room. "Just a minute. That's Vanessa."

She grabbed the phone out of her purse and sank down in her favorite crocheting chair. "Hi, sweetheart!"

"Hi, Mom, how's it going?"

Kate thought about telling her daughter all the things that had happened since she left, but it was just too overwhelming for a phone call. She'd catch Vanessa up when she got home. "Going great. Peter's over, and we're trimming the tree."

"Sounds super. I won't keep you," Vanessa said. "I kind of had something to ask."

Vanessa's hesitant tone immediately sent a spike of worry through Kate. "What's that?"

"You remember Logan Lariby?"

"The actor, of course." Kate kept her tone warm. She liked Vanessa's young friend. She really did. He was amazingly polite and down to earth considering his fame from the movies he'd done. And Logan seemed to treat Vanessa with respect. Still, Kate didn't like the idea of Vanessa getting stars in her eyes over acting.

Not that Vanessa wasn't a lovely girl; Kate knew she was. But there were hundreds of equally lovely girls struggling to find acting jobs. Kate wanted something less risky for her daughter.

"Well, Logan is in New York." Vanessa paused again, clearly unsure of how her next words were going to be taken. "He asked me to come to the city for New Year's Eve to watch the ball drop in Times Square. He's never done it, and he's always wanted to. I know I planned to be home by New Year's Eve, but I have enough time before classes start up again ..." Finally, she just seemed to run out of steam in her rush of words, and she said the last words quietly. "I'd really like to go."

Kate held her breath for a second. She hated the idea of further postponing her gift exchange with Vanessa, but as she listened to her daughter's breathless excitement, she realized something. What she told Harry on the phone was true: Vanessa wasn't a little girl anymore. She was a young woman, and all the choices ahead of her were going to take her farther and farther from Kate. But they only had to come between them if Kate let that happen.

"I think that sounds terrifying," Kate said as soon as she was certain she could speak in a normal tone. "All those people! But it sounds exciting too. I hope you have a wonderful time. Just be careful."

"Really?" The shock was clear in Vanessa's voice. "You don't mind?"

"Logan is a nice young man. He'll make sure you're safe," Kate said. "And you certainly have a good head on your shoulders."

"I mean, you don't mind if I'm gone a few extra days?"

"Mind? I miss you like crazy, but I know you'll be back. We'll get together then."

"Oh, Mom, thank you! I really wouldn't have gone if you wanted me home, but it sounds exciting. I'm going to be in Times Square for New Year's Eve!" she squealed.

"Be careful," Kate repeated. "And don't take anything valuable. A crowd like that is going to be full of pickpockets. And be sure you don't get separated from Logan." Kate turned to see Peter standing with his arms crossed, grinning at her. She made a face at him. "And have fun."

"I will," Vanessa assured her. "And I'll be careful."

They chatted for a bit longer before Vanessa was called away. Kate held the silent phone in her hand for a moment.

"That was very brave of you," Peter said as he stepped closer and touched her shoulder.

"She's growing up," Kate said. "I can't change that." She took a deep breath. "She'll probably do a lot of things that seem crazy dangerous to me. I need to get used to it."

"Speaking as someone who often watches a lady he cares about do crazy dangerous things, you never get used to it."

"And as someone who gets nagged a lot about caution these days," Kate said, "I gained a new perspective."

"I'm never going to stop nagging," he warned before

turning back toward the tree. "Now, surely there are more zombie animals for the tree?"

She swatted his arm. "No there are not. Though once in a craft workshop Vanessa did make a Santa who might look a little like a serial killer."

"I can hardly wait to see."

Twenty

"I'm sorry, I really don't know what to tell you." The clerk at the courthouse looked from Jim to Alice. "The man who officiates at all our weddings isn't going to be back until after Christmas. He went to Houston to spend Christmas with his kids."

Jim had his arm around Alice's waist, and he gave her a squeeze. "It'll be all right, Red," he said gently. "We'll go home to Stony Point as soon as I do the photo shoot in Dallas. We'll get married as soon as we get home. That's not all that long. A couple of weeks. At least all our papers are in order." Even with Jim's effort to sound hearty, the disappointment was clear in his voice.

The clerk helpfully added, "Oh, yes, your papers are fine."

"I just thought it would be nice to be married by Christmas," Alice said softly. She turned to Jim and smiled weakly. "Like our Christmas present to each other."

"I couldn't think of a better present," Jim said. "You know I'm crazy about you." He sighed. "But so far, nothing on this trip has gone according to plan. Why should this?"

Kate saw the misery on Alice's face and felt terrible. She wished desperately that she had something to say that would fix it. She turned to Peter beside her. "You don't happen to know anyone who can perform a wedding, do you?"

Peter shook his head. "The guys I know aren't really the clergy sort."

Kate looked at Alice again. Her friend was blinking much

more than usual, and Kate suspected she was trying not to cry. Suddenly she had an idea. "Wait! I know a judge." She fumbled for her phone and called Rachel Anthony, a judge she had met months before during a photo shoot for one of her books. Kate had helped her find the answer to a terrible secret, and with crocheting as a common interest, they had become friends. She knew Rachel would help now if she could. She tapped her foot as she waited for the phone to connect, then moaned. *Voice mail.* She left a brief message.

"Her phone must be off, but I can keep trying." Kate hated to see the hope fade in Alice's face again. She reached out and touched her friend's arm. "Let me call Vivi. If anyone would have an idea right away, it would be her."

Hope brightened again in Alice's face. "Do you think?"

"It can't hurt to ask." Kate pulled out her phone and called her friend. Her hand trembled slightly as she gripped the phone. She wanted so much to provide a happy ending for Jim and Alice.

"Kate!" Vivi sang out. "How goes the wedding?"

"On hold for the moment," Kate said. "The man who conducts weddings at the courthouse is gone for the holidays. Alice had her heart set on being Mrs. Jim Parker by Christmas. Do you know anyone who could do the ceremony? I tried Rachel, but she's not answering her phone. I haven't given up on her, but I thought I would brainstorm with you over other options." Then a thought flashed through Kate's mind. "How about the pastor from our church?"

"He can't," Vivi said. "Don't you remember? He and his wife were leaving for North Carolina right after the service."

"Oh, right," Kate said sheepishly. Her head had been so full of thoughts of murder and mayhem during the Sunday service that she'd probably missed quite a bit.

"But I do have an uncle," Vivi said. "He's retired from the ministry, but I could call him. He might do it for me."

"Do you think so?" Kate said. The eagerness in her voice must have been contagious because she saw both Alice and Jim perk up.

"I'll call him and call you right back!"

As soon as Kate took the phone away from her ear, Alice and Jim stepped closer. The hope on their faces nearly hurt her heart. "Vivi says she has an uncle who is retired from the ministry. She's going to call to see if he can do the wedding."

"We should wait somewhere more comfortable," Peter suggested. The space around the counter was a little crowded. When they walked out of the clerk's office, Kate was struck again by the historic courthouse's beauty, especially the amazing wrought ironwork. Peter herded them to a bench in the hallway. Alice and Jim sat, but Kate popped back up nearly the instant she touched the bench. "I can't sit," she said apologetically. "Too nervous."

Alice reached out and squeezed her hand. "You're a good friend, Kate Stevens."

"I'm entirely selfish," Kate said. "I really want to be at your wedding."

Alice managed a grin at that. "Hoping to catch the bouquet?" Alice's gaze cut toward Peter, and Kate felt her cheeks flame.

"No," she whispered fiercely.

Alice laughed. "I really want you to be at my wedding too."

When Vivi called back with good news, they all cheered. Vivi's uncle would drive over to Sage Hills to do the wedding at Kate's house. He couldn't come until Christmas Eve, but everyone agreed that would be just perfect.

As soon as Kate hung up the phone, she and Alice looked

at each other, wide-eyed. They had so much to do! The group practically ran out of the courthouse, or as close to a run as Jim could manage with Alice's persistent urging. She and Kate were already calling out lists of things to do as they walked from the pink granite courthouse toward Alice's convertible.

A dove-gray Jaguar pulled up next to the sidewalk just ahead of them. The passenger door opened and Elina Vasin slipped out with the grace of a cat. She smiled at the group as they stopped to look at her in surprise.

The driver's-side door opened and a big man climbed out of the low-slung car to stand in the crook of the open door.

Peter took a step forward, edging ahead of Kate in a not-very-subtle move to shield her. "Miss Vasin," he said. "You can't park there."

She turned a cat-like smile toward him. "I am not parking. I am only pausing." Then her eyes flashed to Kate. "This is the man you prefer to my brother?"

"It isn't a competition," Kate said.

Elina gave her a slightly pitying look. "All of life is a competition. Those who do not realize it are seldom winners."

"May we help you, Miss Vasin?" Peter said, his tone forceful.

She ignored him and turned to look at Alice. "You found John's killer." Alice simply nodded. "I thought you might want to know that I am paying the young woman's legal bills. She now has a *very* good lawyer. I do not believe she will see much time behind bars, which is as it should be. She has a young daughter who needs her. And the world is not so very sad at the loss of this man."

Alice still didn't speak, though Kate saw her posture tighten.

"Murder is always a loss," Peter said.

Elina laughed. "How nice to hear a member of the police who remains an idealist."

"Are you quite done?" Peter asked.

Elina's gaze swept over the group. When her attention turned back to Peter, his posture grew even straighter, if that was possible. Elina smiled. "You think I am going to hurt Kate?"

"I *know* you're not," he said.

Elina laughed. "I like you." She glanced at Kate. "This one is a good choice. Do not worry about my brother. He is already drowning his hurt feelings in the attentions of a completely inappropriate woman. He will not call you again."

"I wasn't worried," Kate said, then immediately wished her voice sounded a little less wobbly.

"Of course not." Again Elina's gaze swept over the group. "Good day to you. And, of course, Merry Christmas."

She folded back into the Jaguar, and the vehicle slipped away.

"Wow, we're not in Stony Point anymore," Alice said quietly.

Jim laughed. "Be careful. She'll get you, my pretty."

Alice turned to smile in his face. "Not before I become Mrs. Jim Parker." Then she laughed out loud. "Come on. We've got a wedding to plan!"

Since the weather had been so mild, especially for those used to New England winters, they made the risky decision to have the wedding in the backyard. By Christmas Eve, the transformation of the backyard was complete. Alice and Kate had run from florist to florist to get the flowers they needed, and Vivi had raided some of the hotel's event decorations. The wedding would have only the smallest of guest lists, of course, but Kate still wanted it to be perfect.

And so, in the early afternoon of Christmas Eve, Kate

stood in her studio, pinning a delicate veil in place over the neat chignon in Alice's hair. Kate had stayed up late the night before, finishing the delicate crochet lace cap that held the tulle. The pattern of the cap matched the delicate crochet bolero-style jacket that Kate had loaned Alice to wear over her green, long-sleeved silk dress. It would offer a little extra warmth in the chilly Texas afternoon.

Just that morning, Kate had woven a small band of fresh flowers that would lie across the seam where the tulle and crochet met. The delicate blue of the flowers fulfilled one wedding tradition for good luck.

"I can't believe you made that," Alice said, her eyes shining. "It's gorgeous."

"And you can't get much newer than a lace cap made last night," Vivi said from the chair where she sat quickly weaving a second band of flowers. This one would go in Kate's hair. The tiny blue flowers matched Kate's long-sleeved crochet dress perfectly. Alice had insisted on the flowers after hearing from Kate about Peter wanting to see flowers in Kate's hair. "So, you have something new and something blue and something borrowed," Vivi said. "What about something old?"

"I have that covered." Alice lifted a delicate necklace away from her neck. "Before I left Stony Point, Annie loaned this to me. It belonged to Betsy. Annie knows I loved her grandmother nearly as much as she did, so it's very special."

"No doubt of that," Kate said as she blinked away the tears that had seemed to keep filling her eyes all morning. Everything was so beautiful and touching. She cleared her throat and tried for a less tearful subject. "Vivi, are you sure your date doesn't mind spending part of his Christmas Eve attending a wedding?"

"Are you sure you want to be back here with us?" Alice

teased. "I saw that hunk of Texas Ranger you came in with."

Vivi grinned impishly. "He said he likes weddings. I think he's really a big ol' mushpot under all that Ranger stiffness. He can talk shop with Peter, and we'll go to his family thing after the wedding. And he says I'm worth the wait."

"Sounds like a keeper," Alice said.

Vivi just shook her head. "It's not serious between us. I'm not sure I'll ever be ready to keep anyone." She frowned at the flowers in her hand. "I think I need more blue. I'll be right back." She hopped up and hurried to the door, peeking through a crack as if she were certain Jim was lurking out there, hoping for a glimpse of the bride. Then she darted through the door, shutting it after her.

Alice turned to Kate. "I want to give you something." She pulled a wrapped package from her overnight bag. Alice had spent the night on Kate's studio daybed to ensure Jim didn't see her before the wedding.

Alice handed the wrapped present to Kate. "I found this in a shop in Atlanta last month. I had to get it for you."

Kate looked at the bright Christmas paper in alarm. "I don't have anything for you."

Alice laughed. "I think this wedding counts as you giving me something. Now don't be silly. Open the present."

Kate carefully peeled the wrapping paper away to reveal a plain cardboard box. When she opened it, she pulled out a mug. On the side of the mug was a drawing of someone completely swathed in scarves and hats so that only the person's eyes peeked out. On the back, the mug read: "Yes, I do crochet. How did you know?"

Kate laughed out loud, and Alice beamed. "See? I finally found a crochet mug."

"I love it." Kate gave her a hug. Then she remembered

how she'd wished only a few days before for another chance to trade crazy gifts with the Hook and Needle Club members. Now here was her Christmas wish fulfilled. "Thanks for making this a fantastic Christmas."

Alice looked at her in surprise. "You like murder and mayhem? Our quiet little Kate?"

"I could do without the murder or mayhem," Kate admitted. "But I can't do without my good friends."

The two women hugged again as Vivi popped back in to finish the flowers for Kate's hair.

As soon as they were ready, Vivi hurried out to change the music on the small stereo she'd brought over. Kate watched from inside as her friend hustled all the men into their places. Then Vivi turned to gesture to Kate to start.

Kate walked out the door and Peter took her arm. She felt her cheeks warm as she peeked sideways at him. He certainly did clean up well in his neat suit and polished cowboy boots.

He leaned in close and whispered, "You wore the flowers in your hair."

"Alice insisted."

"You look beautiful."

Kate was glad of the chill breeze that cooled her flushed cheeks.

He led her to the pastor, who beamed at them with grandfatherly warmth.

Kate took a spot on one side, and Peter stepped over to stand next to Jim. Kate smiled at the clearly nervous photographer, who leaned heavily on his silver cane. "She hasn't changed her mind?" he asked Kate.

She shook her head. "Never in a million years."

The back door opened again, and Jim's gaze snapped in that direction. Alice stepped out. Kate had never seen her friend look lovelier, her cheeks flushed with excitement, her green eyes shining like emeralds.

Jim said something low under his breath. Kate didn't hear it, but judging from the look of awe on the man's face, she was sure it was complimentary. Alice walked to her place and handed the bouquet to Kate so she could take Jim's hands.

The pastor launched into the ceremony with undisguised pleasure. Kate's gaze drifted toward Peter and she saw he was staring at her. The look on his face made Kate's cheeks warm even more.

As the pastor finished the ceremony, Kate saw something white flutter from the sky near her. She gaped in wonder as more white flakes fell. It was snowing! The snow couldn't stick, of course, as the afternoon was far too warm. But the falling flakes settled gently on Jim and Alice as they said their vows, each flake sparkling for an instant before melting.

Kate smiled at the thought that she'd gotten a little New England snow for Christmas after all. Falling snow and a happy ending. What more could she possibly have asked for?